A Thrill
of Hope

A Thrill of Hope

of Hope

KELLYN ROTH

Contents

Dedication

For my mom, who has many good, hard-working, altruistic traits that I unfortunately didn't inherit, and for my dad, who taught me what to look for in a husband.

The Carols of Christmas

In Thy Tender Care
by Courtney Ranger

Watch of Wand'ring Love
by Kendall Hoxsey

Rest Beside The Weary Road
by A. M. Watson

So, To Honor Him
by Alice Monday

Raise the Song on High
by DaLeena Taylor

Beneath the Guiding Star
by Sara A. Thren

And the Mountains in Reply
by Sienna Peake

Of Peace on Earth
by Abigail Kay

A Thrill of Hope
by Kellyn Roth

O Holy Night

O Holy night! The stars are brightly shining
It is the night of our dear Savior's birth
Long lay the world in sin and error pining
'Til He appeared and the soul felt its worth
A thrill of hope the weary world rejoices
For yonder breaks a new and glorious morn
Fall on your knees; O hear the Angel voices!
O night divine, O night when Christ was born
O night, O Holy night, O night divine!

Led by the light of Faith serenely beaming
With glowing hearts by His cradle we stand
So led by light of a star sweetly gleaming
Here come the Wise Men from Orient land
The King of kings lay thus in lowly manger
In all our trials born to be our friend

He knows our need, to our weakness is no stranger
Behold your King; before Him lowly bend
Behold your King; before Him lowly bend

Truly He taught us to love one another;
His law is love and His Gospel is Peace
Chains shall He break, for the slave is our brother
And in His name, all oppression shall cease
Sweet hymns of joy in grateful chorus raise we
Let all within us Praise His Holy name
Christ is the Lord; O praise His name forever!
His power and glory evermore proclaim
His power and glory evermore proclaim

Chapter One

Philadelphia, Pennsylvania
Mid-November 1881

John's head throbbed, but only one letter remained.

The steady scratch of his pen filled the quiet of his small dockside office. Outside, the sounds of the shipping yard along the Delaware River drifted in—workers calling to one another, the creak of wooden crates being loaded, the distant clang of a ship's bell down at the docks. It was the sound of industry. Such noises brought John a deep sense of satisfaction.

He could get more done at the main office of Baldwin & Sons, but he preferred the thick of it here—everyone moving with purpose. It made the world feel more knowable.

November had arrived on a sharp harbor wind, bringing with it pale, cold mornings and the first inescapable stirrings of Christmas. It always started so early ... and it always gave John a headache.

"Johnny."

For a moment, John didn't register the voice, but eventually, it broke through the haze of work reports and a strongly worded missive to a supplier. He looked up and blinked at his father.

"Johnny." His father's eyes were twinkling in that way John particularly disliked. That "I'm about to tell you something about yourself that you're not going to like" way. "It's two."

"Yes?" The middle of the work day? What could Dad possibly have to say about that? "It is indeed."

"Do you remember what you were supposed to be doing at one?"

John sat in silence for a long moment before realization struck and he slowly nodded. "Um. Yes. Yes, I told Mother I would leave at noon and help her unearth boxes of Christmas paraphernalia from the attic for the church. I'll apologize to her." For all his dedication to long hours at the office, he never meant to disrespect his mother. She was practically sainted in their household—his father made sure of it.

"I'm sure she'll recover. I actually went home to eat and helped her." Dad gave him a meaningful look. "Have you eaten today?"

John shrugged. He'd had breakfast, but of course, it being two in the afternoon, that was not what his father meant. "No, but I will soon." John usually did remember to eat—but today, Mother hadn't had Cook pack him a lunch, so he'd forgotten. "I was just wrapping this up." He gestured to the letter in front of him.

Dad laughed and lowered himself heavily into a chair opposite John. "Son, you're becoming a much younger Ebenezer Scrooge."

John picked up his pen. He'd heard this before. "Someone has to be Scrooge, or the world wouldn't go around. It's not like I've kicked any orphans lately; it could be far worse."

His father folded his arms across his chest and frowned. "Now, Johnny—"

"I know, I know." John dropped the poor pen once more and held his hands up. "'The business is thriving; I've done well here; work isn't everything.' It isn't as if I haven't heard this lecture before. You know things will slow down over Christmas. Is it insane to want to get ahead?"

His father's piercing blue gaze still unsettled him, just as it had when he was a boy. John, like his younger brother, resembled Mother in appearance—dark hair, brown eyes—and though his father was generally the cheerier of the two, his eyes *were* particularly keen. "The point is that, though I'm glad you enjoy your work—and I wouldn't have it any other way—what makes it worthwhile if you've no one to come home to?"

John groaned. "Not this again."

"Fine, fine!" Dad grinned; it spread across his round face rather rapidly, as always. "But you know that's what gives life meaning. Family. Now, you have a family in us, but I just think—"

"That I won't have enough meaning until I marry?" John arched an eyebrow. "I'm curious to know what the Apostle Paul would say about that."

Dad inclined his head. "You have a point. Marriage is not the only path to happiness or fulfillment."

"Besides, I'm of the mind that it's too early for me to think about such things." He told himself he had years to decide on marriage, if he decided on it at all.

"You're twenty-three, John. That's older than I was when I married your mother. I doubt this is an age issue."

John blinked. "Perhaps not. In all honesty, I wouldn't even know where to begin."

"With marriage?" his father asked, half-smiling.

John huffed and shook his head. "With any of it. With finding meaning beyond this—" He gestured around his office.

Dad's expression immediately grew serious. "That's simple. Start with your faith. You've been a Christian in name for a long time." His voice wasn't cruel, but John felt the weight of it nonetheless. "But faith isn't meant to be something you claim—it's something you live."

John lowered his gaze, fingers drumming lightly against the desk. He wasn't sure how to respond. "That's not entirely true. I do try. I just ..." *Find it easier to trust in ledgers than in things unseen.* A ship either arrived or it didn't. Answers in faith always seemed far less certain.

He believed. He did. But belief didn't always translate to action, and action was what counted most in the Baldwin family. Taking a deep breath, John did one of the hardest things he ever had to do—which was something, given that he had to do it with some regularity: he asked his father for advice. "What would you do if I were me?"

Dad grinned, probably because he knew he had won, but also, potentially, because he cared about John. "There's any number of things you could try," he said slowly. "Of course, you know what you must do to grow closer to God—talk to Him, read your Bible. But if you wanted something actionable—which knowing you, you do—I would say get more involved at church." He shrugged. "That Christmas bazaar is coming right up. The committee's a mess, and everything's behind." His father shook his head. "Your mother says the whole church is whispering about it. She's not on that committee, but it's adjacent to her projects."

John felt his eyebrows try unsuccessfully to hop off his forehead. "A bazaar? But, Dad, that's ..." He didn't finish the sentence, because there was nothing John Baldwin Sr. hated more than any suggestion that this kind of work was irrelevant. But the truth was, didn't a bazaar matter a lot less? Yes, some of the funds went to good causes, but it was such a frivolous way of raising money. "What are they raising money for this year?"

"Your mother tells me the funds from this bazaar are meant to keep the St. Andrew's Orphanage running through the winter. Is that an important enough cause for you?"

The comment hurt. Of course, his father could read John's Scrooge-like thought. Still, he couldn't see how he fit in. "What do you expect me to do? Bake cakes? I'm not suited for that."

Dad laughed heartily. He had a deep, booming belly-laugh, and the sound tugged a smile from the edges of John's mouth. "The way you are in the kitchen? I wouldn't expose the good people of Philadelphia to that. No, but there's more work that goes into these things than you'd think. There's something for everyone to do."

John shook his head, but once Dad had an idea in his head, it was hard to convince him otherwise. "I suppose I could ask Mother, but I think she'll tell you what I'm thinking." *That I'm the least-quali-fied person in Philadelphia to be involved in a cheery procedure like a Christmas bazaar.*

"I'd ask her, yes, but you should also go to the pastor."

"Fine. I'll speak to him."

His father clapped a warm hand on his shoulder, then turned toward the door. "Good man. You'll be needed. They're scrambling to get everything done in time. They need someone who can get things moving."

"And that's me?" John asked dryly.

"You're good at turning chaos into order."

"Even when the chaos involves tinsel?"

"Especially then."

John sighed and turned back to his letter as his father left the office behind, probably to go terrorize one of the foremen with the invitation to a Baldwin family dinner he'd been avoiding for about six months.

Though John and his father were more different than night and day, in one way, they were the same.

Once they set their sights on a goal, they never gave up.

It was how, Dad always said, a somewhat round, entirely gregarious clerk with determination and a dream had won John's beautiful but austere mother.

John had little in common with his father, but he'd got his stubborn streak, and if the right path to God was through a church bazaar, he'd set his jaw and walk straight through.

Chapter Two

Opening her worn-out leather satchel, Henrietta Miller tucked away the last of the crumpled lists that made up every moment of her waking life. Each scrap was scribbled with reminders, assignments, supplies—everything she hadn't volunteered for but couldn't bring herself to refuse. *Borrowed burdens.* The ironic thought made her want to grimace, but her smile stayed in place, as always, polite and practiced.

A dull throb started behind her eyes. She pinched the bridge of her nose, then smoothed her skirts and forced herself upright, schooling her features into something bright enough to pass.

If anyone noticed how tightly she was moving today, they didn't say a word. And that was the thing about always saying yes—no one ever thought to ask how *you* were managing.

Shoving the notes from today's session on changes to the curriculum for Sunday school down deep, where she would not have to think of them for at least another hour or two, she straightened her back and looked around at the members of the congregation who had met just after church for the annual Christmas bazaar planning meeting. The late afternoon sun cast long, dusty rays through the tall arched windows. Most members of the congregation were already bundling up to leave, their chatter echoing off the high ceiling.

The meeting that was supposed to happen in October. The meeting that, for some reason, everyone had forgotten about.

Was it Henrietta's fault? Should she have reminded people? Perhaps. But she had been so deep in harvest parties and cider gatherings and a Thanksgiving charity event that was mostly planned that she hadn't thought about it.

Not until the pastor approached her that morning and gently, but firmly, remarked that her priorities were out of step with reality.

Her eyes slammed shut, shame burning hot throughout her body. She wouldn't think about that—she would just move forward.

"Henrietta, dear!" Mrs. Leland bustled up to her and pressed a scrap of paper into her hands. "Would you be a dear and pick up these items this week? Perhaps on the way home. You can take what you need from the petty cash. No one else has the time, and we knew you wouldn't mind! It's for the church decorations."

Of course not. Henrietta never minded. She glanced down the list—cloth, ribbons, holly sprigs, more candles. Nothing she couldn't manage, though it might mean rearranging her errands for the week. She forced her smile a little brighter. "Of course, Mrs. Leland. I'll take care of it as soon as I can."

"This is so important for the church," Mrs. Leland proclaimed.

Before she could step away, another voice called her name. "Oh, Henrietta!" She turned to face Mrs. Harper, one of the older ladies, who walked with a limp. "I hate to trouble you, but my rheumatism has been acting up terribly. The only thing that makes me feel a little better is that cream your aunt makes. Would you be so kind as to drop by with some later this week? Perhaps we could visit. It would mean the world to me."

Henrietta hesitated—only for a fraction of a second—but Mrs. Harper's wrinkled hands tightened around hers, her expression hopeful.

Guilt pressed in like a vice. "Of course," Henrietta said softly.

"Bless you, dear girl."

As Mrs. Harper shuffled off, a hand pressed her lightly on her arm. She turned to face Isaiah, a young man of about her age who generally helped her wrangle the younger boys at Sunday school. "What would this church do without you, Henrietta?" Isaiah's voice carried more amusement than admiration, as if her willingness to help was merely a quirk of her personality rather than a burden she carried.

I suppose to anyone else, it is.

But she didn't say that, or let on that she sometimes wished the church didn't rely on her quite as much. Isaiah was the kind of man people naturally gravitated toward—always pleasant, always offering some lighthearted remark that kept conversations easy. She liked Isaiah, but she sometimes wondered how much of his easy manners were pretended, as hers were.

No, she scolded herself. *Not everyone is like you.* Some people were grateful to be alive. *And you ought to be, too.*

"Mark my words, you'll make some man a fine wife one day," Isaiah teased. "Hard to find a young woman as devoted as you. The church would rest easier knowing you settled down."

Henrietta's cheeks burned. It was the sort of comment that made people smirk and glance their way, feeding the ever-growing assumption that she and Isaiah were practically courting.

They weren't courting—not seriously, at least. Yet Henrietta couldn't help but feel trapped by the assumption. Isaiah was safe, steady, and known. But for some reason, she just couldn't do what she knew she was supposed to: namely, give him a sign that his attentions were welcome and expected, as they should be.

So no, their relationship was not serious or exclusive. But no one seemed to notice that small distinction. Not in this church. No, the gossip proved too tempting, and everyone too eager to see two "nice young people" happily married.

She opened her mouth to respond—though what she meant to say, she wasn't sure—but a new voice cut in before she had the chance.

"There you are!"

Henrietta turned just as her cousin Rose slipped through the dwindling crowd, her blue eyes sharp with understanding. She took Henrietta's arm as if they had urgent business elsewhere, offering Isaiah a polite smile. "If you'll excuse us, Isaiah, we must be going."

Isaiah gave a lazy nod. "Of course."

Rose tugged Henrietta away before he could say anything else, steering them toward a quiet alcove near the coatroom. Only when they were out of earshot did Rose sigh. "You can walk away any time you want," she whispered. "Even if it's a church thing. You need a *life*, honey."

Henrietta let out a breath that was half a laugh, half a sigh. "I'm fine."

Rose gave her a knowing look. "You don't have to do everything just because people expect you to."

A lump formed in Henrietta's throat. "I don't mind helping."

"That's not the point." Rose frowned. "You're allowed to say no. People shouldn't just assume you'll do *everything*. Why, no one else would tolerate it!"

Henrietta swallowed hard, which did nothing to ease the pressing guilt. After all, what right did she have to refuse? Her aunt and uncle had opened their home to her after her parents' passing without a moment's hesitation. The least she could do was make herself useful, to earn her keep by being the one who never said no. What other excuse was there for her presence in their lives?

"There you are, Miss Miller."

She turned to find Mrs. Leland again, smiling brightly. "I forgot to mention—you'll be back for the urgent planning meeting tomorrow, won't you?"

Henrietta blinked. No, in truth; at least, she hadn't *known* she would be.

"I just spoke with the pastor—and he said he's sending in Mrs. Baldwin's son, John, to help us organize things for our Christmas Bazaar." Mrs. Leland's nose wrinkled. "I don't see why—but the pastor says he may be able to trim some of the fat." She shrugged. "Odd. I don't know what he could possibly trim."

Henrietta looked up, her brow furrowing. "Does that mean a limited budget?" she asked hesitantly. That couldn't do. The bazaar was the chief delight of her year, and, she presumed, of other people's years as well! Cutting the budget would be criminal, and certainly not the best way to serve the Lord with church funds. "But the bazaar is the heart of this church's charity. Every penny trimmed weakens the good we do."

Mrs. Leland shrugged, unconcerned. "Well, the pastor's orders. We must make do."

Henrietta's fists clenched. Frustration welled, sharp and hot; this felt like a betrayal of the very spirit the bazaar was meant to embody. Why did everything have to be so complicated? The bazaar was already a big enough project, already being started late, and everyone involved was as careful as careful can be with the money. That was always the case with church budgets—they were necessarily tight, and the volunteers found ways to stretch it as far as possible. All proceeds of the bazaar would go to charity, and it was entirely run on donations. While some funds were allotted to it, Henrietta didn't see where any more cuts could be made.

And at the end of the day, the church was not a business. The purpose was not to make a profit. And treating it as such was an affront to not just the church and the bazaar and the people making it happen, but to God Himself.

"We'll see about 'must,'" Henrietta murmured, though mostly to herself. Mrs. Leland, as always, had moved on with barely a parting word.

Chapter Three

J ohn arrived ten minutes early and alone, just as he'd planned. The silence of the church hall calmed him. The cavernous room, empty of its usual Sunday bustle, was faintly scented with candle wax and old floor polish. Rows of empty chairs sat in slight disarray, silent witnesses to yesterday's hasty meeting. He chose the head of the long table. He laid out his notebook with surgical precision, opened to a clean page, and began sharpening each pencil over a folded handkerchief.

This was nothing more than a logistics problem—assignments, timelines, resource allocation. It was almost comforting, really. If he could manage this, it would prove something—to the pastor, to his father. *But I'm not a set of ledgers and expectations in human form. I can do this charity thing, this people thing. I can.*

He could handle this. He could prove to his father that he had skills outside of his normal routine. He *could*, and he *would*.

The door creaked open, and a young woman stepped inside. She was dressed simply and conservatively, but was not unattractive, with blonde ringlets pinned back rather haphazardly and wide brown eyes and a ridiculous smile.

Why was it ridiculous? John wasn't sure. He instinctively knew that it was, though—ridiculous, overblown.

Not real.

John recognized the kind of smile worn by people who were already running late for their next obligation. He stiffened.

She carried an over-stuffed satchel and set it beside a chair in the corner, not at the head of the table. "You must be Mr. Baldwin." She dipped her head in greeting. "I suppose you're here to oversee our little operation?"

John frowned. *Not oversee—serve.* That was the word the pastor had used. "You must be Miss Miller. I know we haven't spoken before, but you know my mother." John had learned early on that mentioning family connections was an easy way to smooth the road.

Unfortunately, this didn't soften Miss Miller's posture or face, like it might have with other women in the church. "Indeed." She took a seat. "I like to be early, to sort through my notes," she said after a beat. "Are you ... That is ... Why are you here?"

John swallowed. He had no notes, but he wasn't about to admit that he'd arrived early to get the lay of the land, soothe his nerves, and, of course, because his habit of pre-meeting note-reviewing was ingrained in him, deeper than his own skin. "I ... misjudged the walk." Wonderful. Now he looked weak: bad at managing time, especially given that he came to this church every Sunday and would know how long the walk was.

Miss Miller blinked then nodded. "I understand you're here to help us 'trim the fat,' as they say," she said, with yet another smile that didn't reach her eyes. "That's the rumor, at least."

John shook his head. Where had she gotten that idea? Not that that hadn't been John's secret thought—there was always waste in these situations—but he wouldn't have put it that way. "No, that is not my intention. My father thought I'd be able to get things ship-shape quicker than most. I know how to complete a complicated project." Did that sound boastful? It did, rather. That wasn't his intention, but it *was* true.

She pulled a sheaf of notes out of her satchel and slapped them on the table with more force than was perhaps necessary, causing the old wooden tabletop to shudder—perhaps with fear at this surprisingly fiery woman. "I only meant that men tend to come in with suggestions and solutions to problems that have already been solved or at least discussed. But since you're here to help, by all means." She slid the papers down the table toward him—handwritten notes, lists, and what looked like a rough sketch of the bazaar layout. "If you want, you can go over this."

John's eye twitched at the lack of structure. Everything was crammed together, with scribbled annotations running into the margins.

He resisted the urge to straighten the papers.

Instead, he picked up a page. "You've got booths assigned, but there's no clear timeline for setup or breakdown."

Miss Miller sighed, rubbing her temple. "I'm working on that."

John flipped to another sheet. "And the budget? Are we tracking expenses?"

"Yes, of course—" Miss Miller pulled out another paper, waving it at him. "But we've had to shift things around since some of the fundraising fell through. I'm *handling* it."

Handling it.

John exhaled through his nose, keeping his expression neutral. "It would be more efficient if we set up a ledger and assigned someone to track spending. For the sake of transparency, this should be someone who has no real stake in the rest of the planning—someone who could be objective. It would help you," he added quickly. "Not 'rein you in.'"

Miss Miller's spine went rigid. Any trace of her practiced smile vanished, leaving her expression utterly blank. Her hands, which had been restlessly sorting through papers, stilled completely on the tabletop. Her gaze, when it finally lifted to his, was flat and cold. She shot him a look. "Would it?" she asked, her voice losing all its previous warmth. "Or would it slow everything down?"

John met her gaze evenly. "A proper budget ensures we don't run out of money before we finish preparations."

She pressed her fingertips to her brow briefly then dropped her hand. "I've *tried*. I promise I've tried. It's just—when three people say they're in charge of the same thing and no one shows up when they're supposed to, it's hard to track anything." She shot him a tired look. "You want a ledger? Fine. But it's not the system that's the problem. It's the people who don't follow it. The truth is, this can't be perfectly structured and businesslike—because it's not about that. It's about people. You have to think of it as what it is—an outpouring of the community, to raise money, yes, but also to help people. Thinking of it as anything less than a center of Christian charity is a mistake of the spirit."

He felt the old burn of being dismissed before he'd even had a chance. He was trying to help—wasn't he? Wasn't this what they'd asked him to do? His jaw tightened. "I'm aware."

"Are you?" She lifted an eyebrow. "Because right now, you're talking about it like a shipping manifest. You're thinking of this too practically."

John inhaled sharply, feeling his patience fray. *This. This* is why he didn't do this kind of thing. It was beyond frustrating. He'd never had a single conversation with a businessman that had included the line 'you're thinking of this too practically.' "And you're treating it as though all will magically fall into place without any sort of legitimate structure."

They stared at each other.

There was the sound of voices in the hall, women talking over and around each other. Through the open door came a group of women, deep in a conversation John didn't hear.

Miss Miller snatched her notes back.

John picked up his pencil.

Chapter Four

Henrietta shoved through the door into the warm kitchen, which always smelled of baked bread and her aunt's floral perfume, and let her satchel thud onto the kitchen table. The beaten-up old thing slumped over, its seams fraying from too many years of faithful service. She knew how it felt.

"Well," Rose said, looking up from her novel, "someone's had a day."

"I've just endured the most frustrating conversation of my life," Henrietta said, pulling off her bonnet and tossing it at a chair. The blue ribbons trailed like they'd given up entirely.

Rose finally glanced up, amusement flickering in her brown eyes. "Oh?"

"Yes. John Baldwin."

That caught Rose's full attention. She straightened. "John Baldwin?"

Henrietta flung herself into the chair across from her cousin. "Yes. The younger, not the elder," she clarified, pressing her hands into her eyes. The headache had been there long before she'd been forced to drag Mr. Baldwin through a bazaar meeting, fighting him every step of the way, but now it had worsened. She feared it might turn into one of her sick headaches, the sort that sometimes left her bedridden. "He's the very serious, very insufferable one."

Rose's lips twitched. Henrietta was annoyed to see that her cousin was trying to bite back a smile. "What did he do?"

Henrietta threw up her hands. "Oh, nothing much—only that he treated me as though I'd never organized a church event in my life. As if I needed him swooping in to fix everything."

Rose hummed thoughtfully, setting her book aside. "Did you tell him off?"

"Oh, in my own way," Henrietta muttered, crossing her arms. "I made it clear that the bazaar is about community and charity, not just numbers and schedules, before the meeting ever started. But that didn't make him any less annoying. I thought he might actually have listened to me, but he didn't." Not that anyone ever did, but every new person who pushed her opinions aside was just as irritating as the last.

Not that she really said anything. At least, not with the ladies at the church.

John Baldwin had already gotten more of a scolding than most people of her acquaintance were likely to receive from her.

He simply had a ... well, a contradictory face.

"Mm-hmm."

"Just because he's good at shipping manifests doesn't mean he understands people. He's about as warm as the ledger books he so adores," Henrietta added, rubbing her eyes. "Though—I suppose he did make a few decent points."

Rose perked up. "Oh?"

"Not that I'd say that to his face. He still has the emotional range of a desk blotter."

"Mmm."

Henrietta crossed her arms. "He's so infuriatingly calm. I just *know* he already decided I was wrong before I said a word."

Rose leaned her chin on her hand, eyes twinkling. "And yet, here you are, ranting about him *instead* of the infamous Isaiah Huckabee. My, my. I had wondered what it would take for you to actually pay a man attention."

Henrietta opened her mouth—then promptly shut it. She'd found these types of accusations were better left unaddressed. The truth was, Henrietta had always found Mr. Baldwin attractive, but that was neither here nor there. She'd never had a conversation with him, so no matter how tall and confident and brown-eyed he was, all of which were things Henrietta particularly admired in a man—and all of which Rose *knew* about—that didn't change the fact that Henrietta was not currently interested in a relationship, and if she were, she would choose someone whose goals aligned with her own.

None of this mattered to Rose, an unrepentant matchmaker despite her own singleness. She simply grinned knowingly.

Henrietta groaned, covering her face with her hands. "Don't look at me like that."

"I'm not looking at you in any way," Rose said, far too innocently.

"Rose, I don't like him. I don't like anyone right now."

"Of course not."

Henrietta dropped her hands onto the table with a sigh. "I can't be bothered with this."

Rose's teasing expression softened. She tilted her head. "Time for what, Henrietta? A man? Or time for anything besides proving you're useful?" When Henrietta didn't answer, Rose pressed gently. "My mother isn't going to put you out on the street if you don't personally ensure every event at church goes off smoothly. You've earned your place here ten times over since she took you in."

Henrietta winced, the truth of Rose's words hitting a little too close to home. "It's not like that at all," she mumbled. "I just don't have time for ridiculous men with their serious faces and their ledgers and their infuriating way of making me question whether I'm actually right about everything."

Rose laughed. "That does sound exhausting."

It was, but then, so was everything else in her life. "Anyway." She stood with a heavy sigh. "I'll be up in our room, trying to organize these schedules. He's given me an abundance of homework. The man will drive me insane. I honestly don't have the time." She patted the frayed edges of her overworked satchel and then hefted it onto her shoulder. "To make this bazaar into anything like what it should be, I'll be up half the night." She hesitated, fingers brushing the satchel. "He wants to cut things. Make it 'efficient.' But it's not about efficiency. If this doesn't feel like Christmas—if people don't feel that joy—then what's the point?" She gave Rose a brittle smile. "Besides, someone has to care enough to make it beautiful."

"Don't forget to stop for supper!" Rose called after Henrietta as she left the room.

Henrietta called a careless "of course" over her shoulder, but in truth, she wasn't sure she could. If she wanted to be ready by Mr. Baldwin's next "emergency" budgeting meeting, which would be with just her and Mrs. Leland, she would have to cram.

Upstairs, she dumped her notes across the small desk and sat staring at them. Scribbles, half-finished lists, a reminder scrawled in the margin: *don't forget baby Jesus blanket.* Why had that ended up on her list? She wasn't even a part of the nativity planning.

Henrietta rested her chin on her palm. Because after all, if she didn't hold it all together, who would?

Chapter Five

As Henrietta entered the church, she found herself immediately greeted by a blast of warmth. There were a few parishioners skirting about today, decorating the chapel for the Christmas season, which was perhaps why this made an ideal public meeting place for Henrietta and Mr. Baldwin. Not that they would be alone—Mrs. Leland would have been present—but it would still be inappropriate for them to meet without others around.

She arrived today with aching arms and an even more aching head, juggling a satchel, a folio of notes, and a basket full of last-minute donations which had been handed to her as she tried to enter the building. Her bonnet had slipped sideways on her curls, and her breath caught from the cold outside. And, of course, she'd barely stepped inside before Mr. Baldwin's voice rang out from the front pews.

"You're late," he called without any further introduction.

He stood behind the table they'd moved into the chapel for planning purposes—today, the meeting room at the back was occupied by a Wednesday prayer meeting. He was flanked by ledgers, neatly stacked papers, and a small pencil case that looked painfully precise.

"Excuse me?"

He gestured to the brass clock mounted on the back wall. "The meeting was scheduled for four o'clock. It's nearly quarter past."

Henrietta clenched her jaw, pushing a curl back beneath her bonnet. "My apologies, Mr. Baldwin. I was delayed by a parishioner who needed assistance." She knew she sounded defensive, but it was the truth—*mostly*. And also, she was tired. Bone-tired. Too tired to explain how much she was already doing.

Mr. Baldwin offered a brief nod and returned to straightening the corner of a ledger. "I've already reviewed the budget," he said, adjusting his cuffs with the kind of tidy efficiency that made Henrietta's nerves twitch. "We'll need to be more mindful of expenditures. I've made a list of necessary purchases and separated out any optional embellishments."

Before Henrietta could respond, Mrs. Leland bustled in through the side door, her hat askew and her hands filled with swatches of ribbon. "I hope you two have started without me—I was waylaid by dear Mrs. Godfrey in the hall, poor thing. Her son's come down with something dreadful. I told her I'd find someone to take care of her duties. Perhaps you could, Henrietta? Oh—but never mind that now. I'll just be a moment—Mrs. Godfrey needs me." Without waiting for a reply, she whirled back out the door, chattering as she went, leaving the two of them in the wide, echoing chapel.

Henrietta watched the door close behind her before exhaling through her nose and setting the donation basket down with a soft thud. "She certainly seems confident in our ability to carry on without her."

Mr. Baldwin did not look up. "If we stay on schedule, it shouldn't be a problem."

Henrietta pulled off her gloves one finger at a time, then stepped to the table. She picked up one of the sheets he'd mentioned. The pencil marks were crisp, categorized with clinical precision.

"You've separated decorations from essentials?"

"Of course," he said, glancing up at her. "The goal is to raise funds, not waste them on things we can do without."

She pursed her lips. "Mr. Baldwin, with all due respect, calling something a waste doesn't make it one. The bazaar isn't simply about revenue. It's about joy, about drawing the community together to celebrate Christmas, to remember why we gather at all."

His brow furrowed faintly, but his voice remained cool. "And none of that matters if we don't stay within the church's financial limits. You said yourself the donations are thinner than expected. I'm simply offering a structure that will help ensure the event succeeds."

"Succeeds by whose standards?" Henrietta challenged. "If it's all columns and counting, perhaps it will be efficient, but it won't be meaningful. People don't come to the bazaar for balance sheets. They come because it feels like Christmas."

"You think we can manufacture that feeling with a few extra garlands?" he asked, his voice raising enough that a young girl walking past glanced at them. He paused, then added in a quieter tone, "This isn't meant to strip it of meaning. It's meant to keep it from collapsing under its own weight."

Henrietta's shoulders tightened. The headache was pressing harder now, curling behind her eyes. "You assume it's a mess. But this event has been running for years. I'm not sure why you think you're the only person who can save it."

"That's not what I said."

"But it's what you implied."

A silence fell between them. Dust swirled in the golden light near the altar, and from somewhere deeper in the church, the faint sound of footsteps echoed—perhaps a janitor or another volunteer arriving late.

Henrietta suddenly felt very cold, despite the warm room.

Mr. Baldwin closed his eyes briefly. When he opened them, he met her gaze evenly. "I'm not trying to diminish what you've done, Miss Miller. I know how hard you've worked. You know my mother does—" made a vague gesture encompassing the hall. "This sort of thing. I know it's difficult and time-consuming and requires certain skills. But I also know we're running short on both time and funds. I thought—perhaps incorrectly—that helping would relieve some of that burden."

Henrietta hesitated. Her hands flattened on the table. "It's not that I don't want help," she admitted, her voice low. "I appreciate that you are taking time to do this. I know you are busy."

He didn't reply for a long moment. Then, slowly, he nodded. "I am busy, but this is how I have chosen to spend my free time. And I want to be useful. I can't be if you don't let me."

"Why?" Henrietta met his eyes and forced another smile. "Why is this what you have chosen?" It didn't make any sense. Clearly, he didn't care about bazaars.

"Because," he said in a firm voice, "I believe my talents *are* needed here. If you could just look beyond your prejudice for a moment, you could see that I am only trying to help."

The chapel door creaked open again, and Mrs. Leland's voice floated back in. "There we are! Oh, good, no bloodshed. Some of us were worried."

Henrietta turned back to her papers.

Mr. Baldwin quietly resumed reviewing the ledger.

Mrs. Leland returned only briefly—just long enough to drop three hymnals on the table, for whatever reason, then swept off in a rustle of skirts. "Back in a moment, dears! Don't wait for me."

Henrietta barely heard her.

She was trying to focus on the column of numbers in front of her, but they kept swimming. The headache that had been stalking her since midmorning had bloomed into something fiercer, the dull pressure curling behind her eyes and pressing into her temples like a vise. She blinked a few times, willing the chapel's warm candlelight to stop flickering, but it didn't help.

Her hand trembled as she lifted her pencil. Not much—just enough to make a crooked mark on the paper. She dropped the pencil with a soft, frustrated sigh and pinched the bridge of her nose.

"Miss Miller?" His voice was abrupt. It always was.

She looked up, startled.

Mr. Baldwin was watching her. Not with the sharp-edged scrutiny he usually wore, but something quieter, more thoughtful.

"Yes?"

"Why are your hands shaking?" he asked.

Henrietta opened her mouth. Closed it again. "They're not."

"They are," he said evenly. "You've blinked hard at least a dozen times in the last two minutes. Your pencil's trembling in your fingers." He paused. "Have you eaten anything today?"

The question caught her off guard.

"I—" She hesitated. Had she? She tried to think. There'd been tea that morning, and half a biscuit someone had pressed into her hand between errands ... but a meal?

"I meant to," she said finally, frowning as she realized how thin that sounded.

Mr. Baldwin didn't say anything for a moment. Then, without

comment, he reached into the small satchel he'd placed beside his stack
of papers and pulled out a neatly wrapped brown-paper parcel.

He pushed it toward her across the table.

Henrietta stared at it. "What is this?"

"Food," he said simply. "Bread, ham, apple slices. My mother insists
on sending more than I need. She knows I forget to eat, and she's
determined not to let me starve to death over a planning meeting at
church. She lives in fear that I'll drop dead at the office."

Henrietta eyed the parcel as if it were an accusation. "I'm not taking
your lunch," she said stiffly, even though her stomach tightened at the
smell of fresh bread.

"You are," he said, and there was no sharpness to his tone now. Just
a kind of quiet certainty. "Because if you don't, you're going to pass
out in the middle of the planning meeting, and then I'll be blamed for
overworking you. Besides, it's not my lunch." He smiled a little too
brightly. "It's my leftovers."

For some reason, this made her laugh, half-hysterically. "I thought
you were trying to convince me to eat it."

"It's all separately packaged." He gave the package another nudge
toward her. "But you're right—that was not appealing. Here, I'll try
again. If I don't eat it, my mother will be disappointed, so please make
it seem as if I did."

Henrietta hesitated another moment. Then, with a soft sigh, she
reached for the parcel and pulled it toward her. "Thank you," she
muttered, not quite meeting his eyes.

Mr. Baldwin only nodded once, briskly, and returned to his papers
as if nothing had happened.

As if he hadn't just noticed something no one else ever did.

As if offering food to someone on the verge of fraying completely
was the most natural thing in the world.

Henrietta peeled open the waxed paper and took a small bite. The bread was soft and buttery, the ham just salty enough to make her stomach growl in betrayal. She ate quickly, neatly, without looking up, feeling more human with each bite.

He didn't glance at her again. He didn't ask if she was feeling better. He didn't make a show of it. Somehow, that made it worse—or better. She wasn't sure which.

Soon, she was back to the rigid numbers on the page, discussing them with the supposedly rigid Mr. Baldwin.

She bent over the ledger again, though her mind lingered on the man beside her, wondering if she had misjudged him.

Chapter Six

The market was chaos.

Children darted between carts, their boots slick with mud from the morning's rain. Merchants shouted their wares in competing tones. Humanity milled here and there, making walking in a straight line impossible. John did not like markets.

He preferred quiet. A dock might be noisy and overcrowded, but there was a sense to it. Besides, John spent most of his time in an office, reviewing ledgers or meeting with businessmen in quiet boardrooms.

But he was here, weaving through the crowd with his overcoat buttoned against the late afternoon chill, a folded list in his pocket, because he was "walking that way." He had meant only to stop by the drug store for his mother's package and perhaps drop by the bookseller for a new penknife. But as he passed the greengrocer, something made him stop.

Henrietta Miller stood just beyond a cart stacked with pine boughs, juggling a too-full basket and what looked like a rapidly unraveling negotiation. Her bonnet had slipped sideways again. A smudge marked her glove—*ink or soot, perhaps?*—and her shoulders were set like a woman holding up the sky.

She was arguing with the stall-keeper. Politely, of course, but with visible strain.

And, as always, she looked tired.

John watched her for a moment, unseen behind a display of turnips. She was working too hard, again. Judging by the faint tremor in her free hand as she reached for a coin purse, she hadn't stopped to eat. *Again.*

She'll work herself into an early grave—and for what? This stupid bazaar? What does it matter in the long term? She's not the only person who can do this. Why does it matter so much to her?

He should have walked away.

Instead, he stepped forward and said, flatly, "You're overpaying."

Miss Miller started like she'd been caught stealing. She turned toward him, her expression a mixture of surprise and exasperation. "What are you doing here?"

"Saving you from spending the church's money unwisely," he replied, nodding toward the overpriced holly.

"I know how to shop, Mr. Baldwin."

"Clearly." He leaned past her and pointed to a second vendor two stalls down. "Their bundles are fuller, and the berries are fresher. You'll pay half as much."

Henrietta narrowed her eyes. "And you just happened to be here at the exact time I'm shopping for the bazaar?"

He hesitated, then cleared his throat. "I'm on an errand for my mother."

Her expression turned unreadable. "I don't need help."

"Of course not," he said, and before she could stop him, he took the basket from her arms. It was heavier than it looked.

"Mr. Baldwin!" she protested, trying to snatch it back.

"It's inefficient for you to carry this alone," he said.

"You're ..." She seemed to search for a word. "Impossible."

"So I've been told. Frequently." He shifted the weight to his left hand. "But I'm still useful." He turned and strode off.

Miss Miller made a sound that could have been either a sigh or a laugh, but she followed him, to John's relief. It would have been awkward if she hadn't.

They passed through the narrow rows of stalls in near silence at first. John purchased the holly sprigs from a different seller at a discount, since it was all for charity. He bought it with his own money—despite Miss Miller's protestation. He felt he had to, after he had made such a fuss about the decorating budget.

Once the sprigs were tucked in the already overflowing basket, Miss Miller raised her eyes to his face with a suspicious look.

"Why are you putting so much energy into this?" she asked. There was a touch of bitterness in her tone. "This is *just* a decoration. And it's not even for the bazaar—Mrs. Leland has me picking these things up for the chapel."

John didn't answer. He didn't know how to explain that he'd spent the last few days wondering whether he'd misjudged her—or whether she'd misjudged him—and that watching her hold herself together with sheer force of will made something twist uncomfortably in his chest.

So instead, he said, "The bazaar will fail if you collapse in the middle of planning it, and I thought this would relieve some stress."

Miss Miller rolled her eyes and turned to the candles at another booth.

"That's because you are good at what you do," he said in a rush.

Miss Miller blinked. "I hope so. You can see—" She gestured about her. "This is most of my life, Mr. Baldwin. It is not easy to have it dismissed."

"I know," he said quickly. "And I'm sorry if that's how it felt."

She nodded and started a conversation about beeswax and its inherent merits.

She was wise. John knew better than to make their conversation personal. After all, what did he know about her? He'd never talked to her before this week, and he probably wouldn't again after the bazaar was over.

Probably.

It was strange that there was even a chance in his mind yet that they would become friends.

Friends, he found himself thinking. *Oh, sure. Dad's going to torment me if he finds out about any of this.*

They continued shopping for another ten minutes, perhaps. He made himself useful, carrying the heavier parcels, fending off one overly aggressive haggler, and once pulling her out of the path of a careening wheelbarrow of squashes.

It happened in a moment. He grabbed her arm and tugged her sharply to the side, just as it shot past. Behind it, the owner shouted an apology.

Miss Miller bumped against his chest, unbalanced for only a moment, but long enough for him to feel startled by how small she was—and how right her arm felt under his hand.

"Are you all right?" he asked hastily.

She looked up, wide-eyed, her curls mussed from the wind and her bonnet askew, as always. "Yes. I—Yes, thank you."

John realized he hadn't let go of her arm. He stepped back immediately, releasing her as if she'd burned him. "Sorry."

She smoothed her skirt, her lips twitching into a look that hovered between amusement and... something else he couldn't quite name. "I suppose that's twice you've saved me this week," she said lightly.

He met her gaze, surprised by the softness in her tone.

"Don't let it go to your head," she added, a little more dryly. But she smiled—really smiled—at him then, and something in John's chest did a small, unfamiliar somersault.

Henrietta turned toward the final vendor on her list.

John followed her in silence, but his thoughts weren't quiet.

At last, her final errand was completed. "I can carry it from here." She gestured to the basket.

John didn't like the thought of her trudging with packages and a basket, along with her beaten satchel, all the way to the church and then home. It would be dark soon. "Let me take the basket to the church and drop it off. It's on my way." *Sort of.* Not entirely. But he wouldn't tell her that.

It took a few minutes to persuade her, but eventually she saw the wisdom and let him go with a quiet thank you and a look of soul-deep relief.

Why is no one taking care of you? he wanted to ask, but he didn't. *Why is no one making sure you're safe and rested?*

Surely that shouldn't be him, but John did like to fix things. He knew that. As he carried Miss Miller's basket back to the church, his thoughts were consumed by her in a way that was new to him. New—and risky.

But perhaps he could feel the situation out. Over the course of the last hour, she hadn't *always* been hostile to him. Perhaps there was a chance she could become ... less so. Perhaps there was a chance she could see him as something more than the great Ruiner of Bazaar Planning.

Maybe there was a chance she could see John.

Chapter Seven

The chapel was already half full when Henrietta stepped through the front doors with her aunt, uncle, and Rose. Her family immediately went to their regular pew but, as always, she had tasks to complete before she could be seated.

She was trying to determine where Mrs. Leland had gotten to today when she spotted Mr. Baldwin. He stood near the rear pews, hands clasped behind his back like a soldier waiting for orders. When he saw her, his mouth tugged into something that wasn't quite a smile—but not quite nothing, either. He looked as if he'd been hoping she might spot him and approached with the ghost of a grin playing about his lips—*unusual for him,* she thought. "Miss Miller," he said. "Good morning."

Henrietta nodded, surprised but not displeased. "Good morning, Mr. Baldwin. You haven't taken a seat?" She noticed the slight nervousness in his posture—how his fingers clutched the gloves he held. *Also strange.* Mr. Baldwin didn't seem the type to fidget.

"No. I generally arrive before my father, but I hate to sit down without my family." He hesitated. "My father and mother are very prompt, but there's always an argument with my younger brother." There was a beat of silence. Then Mr. Baldwin continued, with the faintest edge of awkwardness, "I was going to inquire—about the holly."

She blinked. "Oh. It's holding up nicely, thank you. Looked better than anything I would've found on my own."

"I'm glad," he said, and cleared his throat. "I meant to say this before, but I'm sorry if I've seemed ... difficult. That day at the chapel. I thought I was helping. But I've been thinking—and I believe I was too harsh."

Henrietta cocked her head. Perhaps, but why did he care? "You did help. Really. I think—" She turned slightly, just in time to see Isaiah Huckabee approaching with his usual easy confidence. "Oh, good morning, Isaiah."

Mr. Baldwin followed her gaze.

Henrietta looked from Isaiah to Mr. Baldwin, uncertain. Isaiah's presence always filled a space, and where Mr. Baldwin had just seemed warm, now he looked shuttered.

Isaiah greeted her with a familiar, overbright grin. "Good morning, Henrietta, Baldwin. What have you two to talk about?"

Henrietta frowned slightly. What did it matter to Isaiah? "I saw Mr. Baldwin at the market the other day, when I was picking up some decorations. He ended up helping with some of the heavy lifting. We were talking about that—and about the bazaar."

Mr. Baldwin stiffened slightly beside her. He glanced between them once, and then—too quickly—said, "Yes, it wasn't planned. I ran into Miss Miller by chance. I only helped carry a few things, that was all."

Isaiah raised an eyebrow, amused. "That's mighty decent of you."

Mr. Baldwin nodded, his voice now a little too clipped. "Of course.

I wouldn't have imposed otherwise."

Henrietta was puzzled by the sudden change in tone. She felt like she'd missed something.

But Isaiah just grinned. "Henrietta's always collecting helpers. I guess I've got competition now."

Mr. Baldwin's jaw flexed. "Hardly."

"I'm the one who asked her to save me a seat," Isaiah added, nudging Henrietta gently. "You remembered, right?"

"Oh—I'm helping with the hymnals this morning," Henrietta said, motioning toward the back corner. "Mrs. Langley asked me to reorganize the ones that were misplaced during last week's children's program, and then I also was hoping to catch Mrs. Leland about the Sunday school lesson plans she asked me to copy for her."

Isaiah shrugged. "I'll sit down near the back and wait."

Henrietta didn't bother to tell him that she would be sitting with her family. It did little good to argue, she'd found.

Mr. Baldwin gave a short nod. "Then I suppose I'll take my seat." Before Henrietta could say anything else, he stepped back. His expression was unreadable. He didn't look at her. Not really. It felt as if something fragile had been dropped between them and quietly swept away before she noticed it was missing. "Good day," he said, more to Isaiah than to her, and turned sharply toward a pew on the far side of the sanctuary.

Henrietta frowned slightly. She didn't understand what had just happened—but something had shifted. The warmth from earlier had vanished, replaced with distance. What an odd man he could be.

Isaiah nudged her again. "You all right?"

She forced a smile. "Of course."

But even as Isaiah left her and she resumed her earlier activity of trying to find Mrs. Leland in the crowd, her eyes strayed to the pew where Mr. Baldwin now sat alone, head bowed slightly, hands folded over his knees as if trying very hard not to look at her.

Henrietta wondered what, exactly, she'd said wrong.

John settled into the third pew from the front, right side, the one his family had claimed since before he could read the words in the hymnal. The Baldwin name was etched, figuratively speaking, into this strip of polished wood, worn smooth by years of elbows and shifting Sunday shoes.

He sat with his hands folded, back straight, watching the bright early winter sunlight trickle through the high windows. It was loud in here right now, with everyone talking over each other, a steady buzz of chatter, greetings and conversations bouncing off the high walls. Soon, his parents and younger brother would join him. For now, he had a moment to think. Unfortunately.

He ran a thumb along the edge of his new winter gloves.

Fool.

He'd allowed himself—however briefly, however stupidly—to entertain a notion. An ... inclination. A feeling, perhaps, was the right word. Not even a *plan*, not even anything fully formed. Just the spark of something that might have been interest. He'd admired her stupid satchel full of too many ways she was serving. Her stubbornness. Her kindness, even when worn thin. She'd surprised him. She made him laugh, albeit silently, in ways that unsettled him.

He'd been interested in her. That was all.

But she was spoken for.

John inhaled slowly, pressing the breath deep into his chest and holding it there. He'd heard the whispers about Henrietta Miller and Isaiah Huckabee, same as everyone else. And he'd dismissed them—thought them idle gossip from women who had too much time and too few facts. Henrietta never behaved like she was being courted, and Isaiah was too lazy, too careless, to manage a serious intention. But now ...

I'm the one who looks careless. I barged into a situation I had no business in. He'd inserted himself like an idiot. How she must be laughing at him, John Baldwin Jr., awkward and stilted, daring to think that he might attract the interest of a woman like *that*. She was far too bright and energetic and caring, far too optimistic, far too warm. He wasn't anything like her—he knew he was dull and rigid and stuck in his ways. He knew she would be bored of him if she didn't have to fight with him, which would only last as long as the bazaar planning did. So why had he let himself entertain such a foolish notion?

John couldn't fail to read the way Isaiah had stood beside her—so sure of himself, so comfortable. And Miss Miller hadn't pulled away from his hand on her elbow. Not really. In truth, she hadn't said much at all.

Because she didn't need to. Because she didn't want to. John meant nothing to her, of course; he annoyed her, but there was no spark there, no slight interest.

John adjusted the cuffs of his coat, then his collar, though neither needed fixing. The skin at the back of his neck was warm with embarrassment.

He hadn't even realized, not truly, what he was beginning to feel until just now, when he'd been made to feel foolish for it.

He watched her from across the sanctuary as she knelt near the back, restacking hymnals with careful precision, lips pursed in concentration. She didn't look over. She didn't notice him at all.

Of course not.

That wasn't what this was.

He straightened and folded his hands again, trying to let the familiar rhythm of families finding seats around him settle his soul.

It didn't.

Chapter Eight

"Come, Thou Long-Expected Jesus" echoed off the walls in dozens of raised voices, reverent but bold, as the pastor led the church in one final hymn. Her lips moved, but the words meant little this morning. "Let us find our rest in Thee"—a promise she felt, somehow, did not apply to her. The hymn promised peace, redemption, a Savior to relieve every burden. But Henrietta wasn't sure that applied to the kind of burdens she carried. These were the self-assigned ones. The ones no one ever asked her to bear, but no one stopped her from bearing, either.

Henrietta held the hymnal open between her and Rose, but her eyes barely skimmed the words. Her voice had thinned to a whisper, the notes barely reaching her lips.

It wasn't the first time she'd been distracted in church, but usually, she at least sang the hymns. She could feel Rose watching her.

Rose leaned slightly closer, her voice clear and unbothered. "Something wrong?" she murmured.

Henrietta shook her head, then paused. "I spoke to Mr. Baldwin before church," she said quietly, eyes still fixed ahead.

Rose's lips twitched, but she kept her voice equally low. "Did you, now?"

Henrietta gave a tiny shrug. "Just a brief conversation before the service. He was cold."

Rose cast her a sidelong glance. "Cold how?"

Henrietta frowned. "I don't know. Just different. We were talking, pleasantly enough, and then Isaiah walked up, and—" She hesitated. "He changed."

Rose's eyebrows rose meaningfully. "Changed how?"

Henrietta sighed, adjusting the tilt of the hymnal even though she wasn't reading it. "More formal. Distant. I think he thought ..."

Rose, trying not to smile too obviously in a church pew, leaned in again. "What did you say before he became cold?"

"Nothing," Henrietta said flatly. "It just happened when Isaiah appeared."

Rose gave a soft "hmm" of interest, then, as the final notes of the hymn faded and the congregation began to shift and murmur with the closing benediction, she turned fully toward Henrietta and whispered, "Think of the risks here if you don't do *something*. Do you really want to spend the rest of your life as Henrietta Huckabee?"

Henrietta snorted, trying to mask it with a cough.

"Maybe," she said under her breath. "She sounds like a character in a children's book. Probably talks to geese. I love her already."

Rose gave a soft laugh, but then added more gently, "You know Isaiah would be happy to assume you'll marry him. He's always been good at treating people like a foregone conclusion."

Henrietta's fingers tightened on the hymnal. Isaiah never asked what she wanted. Lately, when he looked at her, all she could feel was the weight of what he expected. So she didn't answer for a moment.

Then, she murmured, "I'm not sure that I want to marry at all." It sounded like another list of tasks to be performed—service that never ended, not even when she could be alone and resting. What would change, really? It would only make things worse. She found herself shuddering at the thought. *Another set of needs to manage, another set of expectations to meet. A husband who expects me to clean and cook and birth and raise children—who expects me to nurture* him *and make* him *comfortable and happy.* People liked her useful. They liked her busy. They liked her when she made things easier for everyone else. She wasn't sure anyone had ever asked what would make things easier for *her*. Surely, a husband wouldn't.

Rose squeezed her elbow as the pastor began the final prayer. "Whatever you do, at least let it be known if you are available. I'd bet my life that's what spooked Mr. Baldwin."

Henrietta ignored her. It didn't matter—not really. She had far more pressing matters on her mind than worrying about whether or not one man or another was interested in her. Adding that stress to her already lengthy list of tasks did not sound pleasant in the slightest.

The storage room beside the church hall smelled faintly of wax and cinnamon soap, with an edge of damp from the stone floor. Crates were stacked in uneven towers against the back wall, and a table sat in the middle, barely visible beneath ribbons, ledgers, scraps of burlap, and a lopsided pile of knitted mittens.

Henrietta pulled her shawl tighter around her shoulders as she crossed to the table, arms full of newly delivered donations. "I think these came from Mrs. Langley. Or possibly her cat."

Mr. Baldwin, already seated at the table with a list in one hand and a half-sorted box of canned preserves in front of him, looked up. He looked pained, an expression that hadn't changed in the last half hour as he tried to make sense of the donations. "They smell like mothballs."

"Then definitely her cat."

She set the box down with a thud. A dusty cloud puffed into the air.

He sneezed. "This is a fire hazard."

Henrietta grinned, reaching for a stack of booth layout sketches and adding them to the cluttered table. "It's tradition."

Mr. Baldwin rubbed the bridge of his nose, his brow pinching. "Tradition is going to kill someone."

Henrietta didn't reply, but her smile lingered as she began unspooling a roll of labels. "If you're looking for order and common sense, you probably shouldn't have signed up to help with the bazaar."

"I didn't sign up," he said dryly. "I was conscripted."

"You offered."

"I was asked."

"You agreed."

"I regret it."

Henrietta laughed softly. "No, you don't."

He didn't respond.

Henrietta had found herself pushing lightly in the last few days, wondering if Rose was right—if there had been genuine interest there, and if she'd ruined it by letting Isaiah presume what Isaiah always presumed.

Yet he'd given her no real sign, despite the fact that he'd been kinder to her. Still John Baldwin Jr.—annoyingly strict, a little too rigid, always trying to plan things in the way that made the most logical sense rather than understanding that placing Mrs. Leland's booth next to Mrs. Langley's booth was not only confusing because of their names, but because they fought constantly.

However, even when he was being himself, Henrietta felt she understood a little more of where he was coming from.

God could do a lot with a man who tried, and Mr. Baldwin was definitely trying.

They both reached for the same box of knitted goods at the same time and hesitated. Henrietta let him take it, her fingers brushing against his. She turned away quickly and began reordering the papers, trying to appear more preoccupied than she felt.

Goodness, though. What had come over her?

A pause stretched between them, quiet but comfortable, filled with the scratch of pencil on paper and the occasional clunk of a tin can landing on the wrong side of the table.

"So," Mr. Baldwin said after a while, "Thanksgiving is next week."

Henrietta hid a smile and nodded. "Typically, it is."

He gave a slight grunt, acknowledging her dry comment. "Where do you go? You live with your aunt and uncle, correct?"

"Yes." She moved to set another box on the table. "My aunt and uncle host most of my aunt's side of the family. He's my father's brother. My mother hadn't much family, you know—that's why I'm here."

He seemed to pause, digesting this information. "Big crowd?"

"Too big." She smiled faintly. "The cousins multiply each year, and someone always burns something. I don't know many of them, and we don't really get a chance to talk at Thanksgiving." She swallowed, unsure if she should tell him she spent the whole day in the kitchen with her aunt and barely knew her uncle's side of the family at all. She barely knew any of her family, outside of Rose. "They can be boisterous. I suppose it's nice."

"Sounds festive."

"It's loud. But I suppose I'd miss it if it weren't."

Mr. Baldwin gave a small nod, still reviewing the booth chart. "I don't envy you. It's only the four of us, now that the grandparents have passed on, and we struggle to pull just us four through the daily events. My family has a rigid schedule: prayer, turkey, argument, pie."

She smothered a laugh. "What's the argument about?"

He arched a brow. "What *isn't* it about?" He cleared his throat. "Speaking of family and who is and isn't at Thanksgiving—" He hesitated. "When do you expect things to be settled with you and Huckabee?"

Henrietta froze, her hand hovering over a stack of jar labels. "I didn't realize there was anything to settle."

He looked slightly startled. "Oh. I only meant—I assumed—I'm sorry. That was inappropriate, wasn't it?" He straightened. "My mother says I tend to ask more than I'm really allowed to know."

She busied herself with a twist of ribbon. "It's all right."

"I didn't mean to overstep."

Henrietta's voice was calm, but her movements were clipped. "It's nothing you haven't heard from half the church by now. You didn't assume anything everyone else hasn't."

He said nothing. She could feel him watching her as she tied a ribbon a little too tightly around a jar of peach preserves.

Finally, Mr. Baldwin spoke again—quietly. "Do you have a date set? I thought it wasn't *official* because you don't have a ring, but I suppose not everyone wears one. I'm sorry if I've offended you. I'm sure everything is as it should be."

Henrietta blinked. *Oh.* He thought that she meant they were en-gaged—not that there was no "settling things" at all. "We're not engaged," she said quickly. "He hasn't asked me."

"Ah." Then he just stared at her for an unnervingly long moment. Then, oddly enough, he smiled. A slow, sort of smug smile. "So ... you're technically still available."

She looked away, unable to hold his gaze. Honestly, she wasn't sure how she felt about the implication there, and she had no idea how she could reply to that question.

Outside the side room, voices rose—laughter and the clatter of more donations arriving. The moment passed.

Henrietta turned back to her list. "We should decide whether Booth Four can be combined with the ornaments table. It doesn't look like we'll have enough to fill both."

Mr. Baldwin simply nodded. "Booth Four's table is warped anyway. Might be a mercy."

Henrietta nodded and ran outside to collect the next box of donations. For a moment, she paused and pressed her cool hands to her hot cheeks.

*Good*ness, *that* smirk.

Chapter Nine

T he Baldwin home was quieter now, the argument of the year having finally sputtered out somewhere between the stuffing and the gravy boat. In its place was the lull that came just before dessert—when stomachs were too full to move and family dynamics were temporarily at peace.

John sat in his usual chair near the hearth, nursing a second cup of coffee he didn't need. Across the room, his mother was humming to herself as she flipped through a magazine. His father was telling a story no one had asked for about a failed turkey hunt in his youth, and Rupert was sprawled sideways in the armchair, one leg dangling over the side, a book over his face.

John was, for the moment, content. Full. Calm. Almost warm, even, though he still hadn't taken off his waistcoat.

"You know," he said, half to himself, "Miss Miller mentioned that her aunt and uncle host Thanksgiving for most of her family. Mother, do you know the Millers?"

Three heads turned toward him with near-identical expressions of glee.

His father grinned. "Oh-ho. *Miss Miller*, is it?"

John didn't look up from his coffee. "She works on the church bazaar committee. We've been coordinating. I was curious."

"Oh, curious, he says," Rupert said with a snort, sitting up and tossing his serial aside. "This from the man who didn't even notice when Miss Jones was hanging off his arm all last spring."

"Or was that Miss Eliot?" Mother asked.

"I don't remember either of them," John muttered.

"Exactly," Rupert said.

John tried to redirect. "She's lived here a while, hasn't she? Her uncle is Joseph Miller, I think."

His mother nodded, easing into the rocking chair beside the hearth with a satisfied sigh. "Yes, Joseph and Lydia. He's your Uncle Richard's solicitor, I believe. A good man. His wife is a bit nervous, but she's always kind. As for Miss Miller—she's been with them for ... goodness, it must be nearly ten years now."

"She lost her parents young, didn't she?" John asked.

Mother's expression softened. "Yes, her mother passed when she was a child, and then her father just a few years later—consumption, I believe. She went to live with the Millers not long after that. It was a difficult time, but she never made a fuss. Always helpful, always in the kitchen or assisting the older ladies at church. She practically raised her cousin, that younger one—Rose."

"She's the one with the laugh," Rupert offered helpfully.

"They both laugh," Dad said.

"No, but hers sort of—echoes. You can hear it across the building," Rupert explained. "I don't know that I've heard her cousin laugh, though."

"Thank you, Rupert," John said dryly.

"Well, I like her," Dad announced. "The older one. What's her name again?"

"Henrietta," Mother supplied, shooting her husband a fond look.

"Right, right. Henrietta. She's got grit. I remember seeing her out with the Huckabee boy, and she looked about as impressed as a cat in the rain."

Mother raised a brow. "I didn't know she was walking out with Isaiah Huckabee."

"She isn't," John said quickly.

Three pairs of eyebrows rose in unison.

"*Isn't* she?" his mother asked delicately.

"I thought she was," Rupert said. "Everyone at church says so."

"Well, they're wrong," John said, then instantly regretted sounding so definite. He cleared his throat. "I mean—there's no announcement. No ring. She told me they're not engaged."

"Told you?" Rupert crowed.

"Would you like some pie, Rupert?" John asked coolly. "I could put it directly in your face."

Mother laughed, rocking gently. "Oh, John. I've never seen you so defensive. Do you like her?"

John took another sip of coffee. "I'm trying to decide."

There was a beat of silence. Then his father burst out laughing.

Mother shook her head fondly. "Well, I don't blame you. She's a dear girl. A bit overworked, I always thought. You could help her with that—though I'm not sure how *you* could convince anyone to work *less*."

Rupert leaned back, folding his arms behind his head. "If you don't ask her to walk with you soon, someone else will."

"I'm not asking her to walk with me," John said.

"No, no, of course not," his father said, mock-serious. "You're simply inquiring after her extended family history out of sheer civic curiosity. Very noble."

John rubbed the bridge of his nose. "I should have asked after the pie."

"Too late now," Rupert said smugly, a big grin stretching his wide face. "You've given yourself away."

Mother rose and patted John's shoulder as she passed. "If you do decide, dear," she said gently, "I think she'd be lucky to have you."

John said nothing. But as his mother disappeared into the kitchen, and his father launched into yet another story, and Rupert resumed his absurd slouch, he felt the corners of his mouth twitch upward.

Just slightly.

Once the pie was brought out, John hoped his father would be too preoccupied with the dessert to continue teasing him. Unfortunately, he was wrong.

"You know," Dad said in between bites, "this Isaiah Huckabee might be interested in her, but that isn't an indication that she's not available. Your mother was engaged when I met her."

"Oh, darling, please," Mother protested.

"You were?" Rupert asked, nearly dropping his fork.

"I was," Mother said, coolly, smoothing her napkin over her lap. "It was a perfectly respectable match. On paper."

Dad chuckled. "Respectable, maybe. But dull as boiled cabbage."

Mother didn't argue.

"I never expected to like your father," she said, with a little shrug. "He wasn't the sort of man I had in mind. And I certainly wasn't the sort of girl he'd—well, never mind that."

"She was," Dad said with a grin, "the prettiest girl in three counties. And don't let her pretend otherwise. Bright, elegant, knew exactly what to say at every gathering. All the fellas were tripping over themselves to carry her gloves or pass her a plate of sandwiches."

Mother gave him a sidelong glance. "And you, as I recall, were not one of them."

"No," Dad said, spreading his hands. "I had a shipping business to run. No time to fawn. Besides, I figured if I was going to impress her, it wouldn't be by acting like everyone else."

"He was persistent," Mother admitted. "Not annoying or aggressive. But he was always there, somehow, whenever I needed him."

"I had goals," Dad said, leaning forward now. "Big ones. Your grandfather's business was solid, but I wanted more—more routes, more contracts, better ships. I knew where I was going, and I wanted a woman beside me who wouldn't flinch at the work it would take."

Mother smiled faintly. "And I was surprised when I found I wanted to be that woman."

Rupert groaned. "This is disgustingly romantic."

John snorted.

Dad grinned. "What, you don't want your old man giving you hope?"

"I don't want to hope," John said dryly. "I'm not sure I'm interested in her."

Mother's tone turned teasing. "You're the one asking about Henrietta Miller's background, dear. We're simply offering perspective."

Dad leaned back, folding his hands over his stomach. "All I'm saying is, an engagement doesn't mean much until there's a ring on a finger and a date on the calendar."

Mother arched a brow. "And sometimes, not even then."

"Exactly." Dad winked at John. "Sometimes the most elegant, untouchable girl in the room ends up choosing the man no one expected. Confidence, sincerity, and good humor go a long way."

Rupert jabbed a thumb at their father. "He's talking about himself again, in case you missed it."

John rolled his eyes, but the edges of his mouth curled in spite of himself.

Chapter Ten

Henrietta stood at the base of a ladder as Mr. Baldwin adjusted the last strand of garland above the front arch of the sanctuary. Frankly, she wasn't sure why Mr. Baldwin had agreed to help her with this—but she was glad he had. She had been concerned about climbing those rungs again, and though she'd intended to finish decorating before their meeting, there hadn't been time.

"Higher on the left," she called, voice echoing in the near-empty room. There were parishioners scurrying about from time to time, so they weren't completely alone, but they were *working* alone, as they so often had recently. After their meeting, when Henrietta had admitted she was staying to finish the decorations, Mr. Baldwin had offered to stay.

Mr. Baldwin nudged the greenery, then looked down. "Better?"

She stepped back, tilted her head, and smiled. "Perfect."

He climbed down slowly, brushing pine needles off his coat. "That's the last of it, then."

She nodded. "Thank you. I'd still be here next Thursday trying to untangle ribbon if you hadn't stayed."

"You would've managed."

"I would've *cried*. *Then* managed."

Mr. Baldwin gave a quiet huff of laughter, then fell silent. Henrietta glanced up and found him watching her intently. His long, steady look gave her the impression that perhaps, just perhaps, he was seeing *her*—not as a list of tasks or a fellow committee member, but as a person.

As a woman, maybe?

Her pulse ticked up.

"I'm not very good at this," Mr. Baldwin said suddenly.

"At decorating?" she asked, half-teasing. He could at least follow instructions, which was more than she could say for some men.

He shook his head. "At talking."

Henrietta smiled. "You do fine."

"I just never know when I'm saying the wrong thing." He cleared his throat, stepping a little closer. "But I know I like being here with you. I don't think I've said that."

The silence grew.

Henrietta looked down at her hands. "You didn't have to."

She felt him beside her before she looked up again—close enough to feel the warmth of him in the too-still sanctuary.

Their eyes met.

For a moment, the church felt like it belonged only to them. Her breath caught. She saw the question in his eyes.

"Henrietta?" The voice rang out from the entry hall, sharp and chipper.

Henrietta startled and took a step back, brushing her skirt smooth. Mr. Baldwin turned away, jaw tense.

Mrs. Dawsey's heels clicked closer on the church floor.

"I thought I'd find you two here," she chirped, rounding the corner with a bundle of programs in her hands. "I'm dropping these off for Sunday—oh, how lovely! I didn't know we had such capable decorators!"

Henrietta forced a smile. "Just finishing up."

"Wonderful, wonderful," Mrs. Dawsey said, bustling past them. "And how very nice to see the two of you working together. I do love to see young people take initiative!"

Mr. Baldwin gave a short, polite nod. "Yes, ma'am."

Henrietta's face was warm.

As Mrs. Dawsey disappeared into the side office, Mr. Baldwin looked at Henrietta again—this time more carefully guarded.

"I should go," he said. "It's late."

She nodded.

He hesitated, then picked up his coat and walked slowly toward the side exit.

Henrietta let out a slow breath and turned to collect her things. She should be going home, too.

There was much to do before she could go to bed.

But still, the memory of that moment would not leave her.

Was he thinking about ... kissing *me?*

Surely not! And yet the thought didn't leave her on the walk home.

Henrietta let herself into the parlor of her aunt and uncle's house quietly, loosening her shawl with one hand and rubbing the back of her neck with the other. She didn't realize how tense she'd been until the warmth of home began to unspool every nerve in her body.

Rose sat on the settee with her legs curled beneath her and a book open in her lap, though she wasn't reading. She looked up as the door clicked shut. "You're home late."

Henrietta nodded, draping her shawl over a nearby chair. "Things ran long. We had to sort through more than I thought."

"Booth prep?"

Henrietta shrugged. "Ribbons and ribbons."

Rose offered a faint smile, but her gaze lingered. "You look like you've been thinking too hard."

Henrietta made a sound that wasn't *quite* agreement but wasn't denial either. She crossed the room and lowered herself onto the armchair near the fire, rubbing her palms together out of habit more than cold.

Rose closed her book and set it aside. "Long day?"

Henrietta hesitated, then nodded. "Yes."

She didn't elaborate, and Rose didn't push—at first.

"I suppose Mr. Baldwin was helping again?" she asked after a pause, as casually as one might ask about the weather.

Henrietta glanced up. "He was."

More silence. Then Rose arched a brow. "You always get that look when you talk about him."

Henrietta blinked. "What look?"

"That *look*," Rose said, motioning vaguely.

Henrietta exhaled a breath somewhere between a laugh and a sigh. "I'm not entirely sure, but I think we almost kissed today."

Rose sat upright. "You what?"

"*Almost*," Henrietta clarified quickly. "He didn't. Someone came in, and that was the end of it."

Rose stared at her. "That's unexpected."

"It was." Henrietta twisted her hands in her lap. "It doesn't mean anything. It's just attraction, I suppose. I wasn't sure, though—we didn't talk about it, so how is a girl to know? Honestly, this is so frustrating."

Rose didn't argue. "Do *you* want it to mean something?"

Henrietta's face lit up in flames. "He's kind. He doesn't talk much, but I feel he understands me. My typical scatter-brained nonsense doesn't seem to change his manner toward me. With him, I can be quiet or tired or messy, and he won't stop respecting me."

Rose's expression softened. "That's not *nothing*, Henrietta."

Henrietta wasn't sure. She was so unused to any male attention beyond Isaiah's—and Isaiah was so honest, so forward. Mr. Baldwin was ... nothing like Isaiah at all. In a good way. "I just wish I knew what *he* wanted," she said. "He's impossible to read. One moment, he's warm. The next, he's backing away like I've startled him."

"Maybe you have," Rose said gently. "Maybe you're unexpected for him, too."

Henrietta gave her a sharp glance.

"I meant that as a compliment," Rose added with a dry smile. "You're too real for a man who's only ever been on the edges of things. Everyone talks about it—he's so withdrawn. Maybe he doesn't know how to handle a potential relationship. You might not be the only one who's unsure, after all!"

Henrietta said nothing.

After a pause, Rose added, "What about Isaiah?"

Henrietta frowned. "What about him?"

"Well, the rest of the church is just about writing your wedding invitations."

"I'm not." Her voice was flat.

Rose nodded. "Then you might want to make that abundantly

clear before someone gets hurt. Isaiah—or you—or John Baldwin, for that matter."

Henrietta didn't reply. Her gaze drifted back to the fire, to the slow burn of flame curling around wood. She was tired—of questions, of assumptions, of feeling like her choices weren't hers. The flicker of wanting something different felt almost brave.

Chapter Eleven

The holiday season was in full swing, and as the days grew colder, the preparations for the annual church bazaar ramped up. The church was buzzing with energy—everyone was focused on their tasks, from organizing the booths to ensuring the refreshments were ordered in time. John had found himself increasingly immersed in the event's logistics.

In truth, though he had initially agreed to help out of duty to his father, he'd begun to take the project much more seriously. He saw now how much this event meant to the church.

How much it meant to Miss Miller.

A chilling thought, that one.

In truth, though, that hardly mattered. John had no indication she had any feelings for him, after all. Even if he had felt something—something different, something he'd not experienced before—she'd given him no sign she felt the same. Therefore, John must batten down his impulses, and simply focus on making sure the bazaar went off well.

It was one of those chilly December mornings when John found himself at the church again, looking over the final list of items for the bazaar. Miss Miller was nearby, speaking with a few other women, and as always, she seemed to be juggling five different projects. Quite a few different events seemed to be in the final planning stages, and Miss Miller, with her typical forced enthusiasm, was fielding questions from practically everyone all at once.

John couldn't help but notice the dark circles under her eyes, the slight tremor of her hands whenever she released her grip on that horrid battered satchel she tugged around with her everywhere—she had been working tirelessly, not just at the bazaar but also in fulfilling the expectations placed on her by everyone else.

He watched her for a moment, his brow furrowing in thought. It was strange, this feeling he had whenever he saw her—almost like he was seeing her for the first time, not as the girl from church who was always too busy to pay attention to him, but as someone he actually wanted to get to know better.

As if sensing his gaze, Miss Miller turned, and their eyes met across the room. A quick, fleeting smile passed between them, and something shifted in the air as it always did between them now. Something new.

But was it scary new or good new? John wasn't sure yet.

Miss Miller excused herself from the group she was with and walked toward him. "I was just telling the ladies we could use some more volunteers for setup. Do you know if we've got enough volunteers lined up for that?"

John hesitated, considering her question but also seeing how she looked—flyaway hairs escaping her bun, a visual cue that she was fraying at the edges. He had seen this before, and the sight of it unsettled him more than it ever had before.

"I'll speak with a few of the women and see who can remove that from your list," he said, perhaps more firmly than he'd intended. "You've already done more than enough. It isn't fair for you to do this, too."

Miss Miller blinked. "I—thank you," she said slowly, as if she couldn't quite believe anyone would care to take a task away from her instead of adding to her massive to-do list. "But we all have our part to play."

"I know," he said, then lowered his voice a pitch. "But you've been doing more than your fair share, don't you think?" He tried to keep his voice light, not challenging her authority in these matters as he might have once. No, instead, he wanted her to know he cared—that her work was important, but so was her rest, her joy, her peace of mind. *Why doesn't she see that for herself?* It didn't matter. John saw it.

Miss Miller gave him a small smile, but there was something in her eyes that made him think she didn't entirely believe him. "I'm fine. Really. It's just that ... well, everyone depends on me to keep things running smoothly."

John felt a pang of frustration at the way she dismissed herself so easily, as if she were afraid to accept help or even rest. "Unfortunately, you are a human being. Sometimes you have to rest. You're not an automaton."

She looked at him, her gaze soft but tinged with something like sadness. "I know," she said. "But if I don't do it, who will?"

Before he could respond, another group of people entered the church hall, mostly young men, and Miss Miller turned to them, her expression shifting back to the strained mask of cheerfulness she always wore as she began organizing her troops like a small but vastly overburdened general. A few words from her indicated to John that this was the group she'd been hoping would help with setup, and they had come to receive orders.

Amongst them was Isaiah Huckabee. The man immediately shifted to her side, interrupting whatever she was saying.

John seethed, but there was nothing he could do about it. The church gossip was that Henrietta and Isaiah were a couple—or practically. John had no place coming in between them. Did he?

But what if Isaiah was interfering with the integrity of the event by pretending to know more than he did? That might be a different situation entirely.

Isaiah was leaning over Miss Miller's shoulder now, looking at one of her abundant lists—this one probably a duty roster—that she was attempting to read to the men in front of her. "Henrietta," he said, cutting through her words once again, "you've arranged the schedule for setting up the booths and decorations—but what about cleanup afterward? You wouldn't want the ladies to arrive Sunday morning to a mess, would you?"

Miss Miller froze. A flush rose to her cheeks. "Oh—I forgot to—of course, we'll need to ..." She fumbled with the notes in her satchel, clearly mortified.

John's heart clenched. *I know you had a plan for that, even if you lost it in the rush of everything. Don't let him fluster you. You're doing so much.* But of course, Miss Miller couldn't hear his thoughts. *Your defense is useless to her unless it's spoken, you fool.*

"I'll put together a list," she said, looking up at the men. "Perhaps—"

Isaiah chuckled, clapping her lightly on the shoulder as if it were all a joke. "No need to worry. You're already handling everything else. What's one more list for our tireless Miss Miller? She can manage it."

A ripple of condescending laughter passed through the group. Several men nodded as if it were a perfectly natural expectation. Miss Miller forced a smile, but her hands twisted the strap of her satchel in a nervous knot.

That was it. How dare they tease her? She was already doing far, far too much! It wasn't fair. John stepped forward. "Actually, no. She cannot manage it. She has already taken on far too much."

The men looked at him in surprise. Miss Miller's eyes widened, though John couldn't tell if it was from relief or embarrassment.

He went on evenly, "Cleanup is not a one-person task, nor is organizing it. I'll draw up a rota with the other men. That way the burden doesn't fall on one person's shoulders. Miss Miller has done her part—more than her part."

A hush fell. Isaiah shifted uncomfortably, his grin faltering. "Well, if you feel so strongly, Baldwin ..."

"I do," John said simply.

One by one, the young men nodded. Someone muttered, "Makes sense," and the tension broke as the group returned to discussing details.

But John caught the flicker of Miss Miller's gaze—shaken, grateful, uncertain, embarrassed—before she turned back to her satchel.

And he knew the whispers about what exactly Miss Henrietta Miller meant to Mr. John Baldwin Jr. would spread before long.

Chapter Twelve

T he last of the young men clattered out into the cold, their laughter spilling into the night air. Henrietta lingered by the door, clutching her shawl about her shoulders as if she could draw strength from the folds of wool. She had dismissed them briskly, but now that she stood still, the silence pressed heavy.

What was that all about?

No one ever came to her defense. Ever. Least of all, a man like Mr. Baldwin, who had originally been so irritated with her and her rather roundabout methods of getting things done. It was unnerving to realize he had been watching her so closely.

But not unnerving like "I'm being watched by someone whose attention I don't want." Unnerving like "I can't believe he noticed me." Unnerving like "Am I really important to him?" Unnerving like "Is this just how he treats all women, or is it just me?" Unnerving like "How will I respond if he is interested in me—romantically or otherwise?"

She was still standing out in the softly drifting snow, struggling to sort through these feelings, which were marvelously unexpected, when Mr. Baldwin stepped out behind her.

He hovered a few steps away from her, obviously wanting to approach her but not knowing what to say, awkward in his stance, his hat twisting in his hands. When she finally turned and acknowledged him with an inclination of her head, he cleared his throat.

"Miss Miller."

"Mr. Baldwin."

"Are you going home now?"

"I am."

He nodded then glanced about, taking in the cold and rapidly emptying street. Almost everyone had disappeared save those staying behind for the choir practice, which Henrietta had excused herself from just this once, claiming a sore throat—which was half-true. "Allow me to see you home."

"That isn't necessary," she said too quickly, though her voice wavered. "It's only a short walk, and I'll be fine. Your home is in a different direction; it would be too much of an inconvenience."

"It's dark and icy," Mr. Baldwin replied, his tone firmer than his usual reserve allowed. He gestured toward the steps. "At least as far as your uncle's gate. Unless—" He hesitated. "Unless you would rather I not. Truly. I don't mean to force my attentions on you, Miss Miller. If I ever seem to, please let me know so I can rectify that error at once."

Henrietta gulped. Though he said the words in a nonchalant manner, she was sure there was an underlying meaning to them. The sort of depth Isaiah Huckabee couldn't begin to comprehend.

She wavered, pride and weariness warring, then relented with a quiet, "Very well. I would appreciate that." She wasn't ready to address anything further than that.

"Let me take your satchel." He held out his hand.

Henrietta swallowed reflexively. She almost never let anyone touch her satchel. But, slowly and reluctantly, she placed it in his hand. After all, he couldn't be kept from doing the gentlemanly thing, could he?

They descended into the frosty night. The air smelled of chimney smoke and pine, their footsteps crunching on frozen earth. For several paces neither spoke. Henrietta's mind replayed the humiliating moment—Isaiah's laugh, the careless burden he had heaped upon her, and then Mr. Baldwin's unexpected protest.

"I—I ought to have remembered about the cleaning," she said at last, voice low. "It was my oversight. I know I have that list somewhere, but I have no idea where it got to, or what it said. And it was my responsibility, anyway, or it should have been. Everyone knows I've always completed the volunteer lists for the bazaar."

"No," Mr. Baldwin said, again in that calculated composure. "It was too much already. Huckabee had no business adding more."

She flushed, staring at the ground. "But it was my responsibility. If I were better organized—"

"You're already carrying more than anyone should have to." His voice softened, but there was an edge beneath it, a restrained anger not aimed at her. "It isn't a lack of organization. I thought that was it, but it's not. Like it or not, you are not bad at these things, Miss Miller. In fact, you have a unique talent for them. It's that everyone expects you to do the work of ten people, and you never refuse."

Henrietta stopped short, then turned her face away, lest the lamplight catch the sheen of unshed tears in her eyes. It wouldn't do for him to see those. "What else should I do? If I don't step in, things fall apart."

Mr. Baldwin turned to face her fully, the chill reddening his cheeks. "Then let them fall apart. At least once. Perhaps people will finally see how much they've relied upon you ... and then things will change for the better."

Her breath caught. No one had ever spoken such words to her—not in defense, not with such certainty. She gripped her shawl tighter, as if to hold herself together. "That isn't how the world works," she whispered. "If I stop, everything stops."

Mr. Baldwin studied her for a long moment, his expression unreadable in the shadows. Then he said, almost gently, "Maybe not everything. Maybe just the things that were never meant for you to carry—that perhaps, were never meant to happen, if it meant your suffering. You weren't built for suffering, were you, Miss Miller? Surely all of us were built for joy—great joy—God's joy. You can't possibly be the first of God's creations that He built with non-stop work and no rest in mind."

Henrietta could not answer. Her throat ached. They walked the remaining distance in silence, though the quiet between them was full—of things unspoken, of warmth and unease, of something like hope that terrified her more than exhaustion ever had.

At her uncle's gate, she turned quickly, forcing composure into her voice, as she held out her hand for her leather bag. "Thank you, Mr. Baldwin. Good night."

He handed her the satchel and inclined his head, as solemn as if he had escorted a queen. "Good night, Miss Miller."

Only when she slipped through the gate and closed it behind her did she let herself sag against the post, trembling—not from the cold, but from the way he had looked at her, as though her work was not what defined her.

How odd to be someone other than Henrietta Miller, the church volunteer.

How strange to be, perhaps, Henrietta Miller—a woman who a man like John Baldwin might walk home with.

Chapter Thirteen

For a long moment, she stood at the gate, after Mr. Baldwin had disappeared into the darkness, and thought, until her fingers' numbness and the persistent ache of her throat drove her up the path and onto the porch. She slipped through the front door as quietly as she could manage, brushing the clinging flakes of snow from her shawl with her free hand. The familiar scent of coal smoke and baked apples wrapped around her, comforting and ordinary—so unlike the storm inside her chest. She had hoped to steal up the staircase unnoticed, but her uncle's voice reached her from the sitting room.

"You're later than usual, Henrietta."

She froze, then forced herself into the doorway. Her uncle sat in his armchair, spectacles perched low on his nose as he studied a newspaper. A lamp glowed warmly at his elbow; it appeared her aunt was nowhere to be seen, but that probably meant she was in the kitchen, based on the apple pie smells drifting about the house.

"It was a long meeting," she said, perhaps a little too quickly—too defensively. In truth, there was nothing to hide, but Mr. Baldwin had unsettled her, and she wasn't sure how to share it with her family, or even if it was worth sharing about. Perhaps it was. Perhaps it was all in her head.

But he certainly seems to like me—and to pay attention to me. Oh, Lord, what is he thinking? Why couldn't we just have kept bickering about our stupid lists and kept the complications at a minimum? Henrietta was far too tired to try to understand anything of what was passing between them.

Uncle Joseph slowly but deliberately folded the paper and eyed her with mild curiosity. "I thought the meeting ended an hour ago. I passed several women who would have been at the meeting on my way home from work."

Henrietta swallowed. "Yes, well ... there was some trouble with the volunteer lists. I had to assign someone to handle it." She tugged at the fringe of her shawl and swung her satchel back and forth with the free hand, wishing she could smooth the heat from her cheeks as easily. "Delegating tasks always takes longer than I think it will." Which was another reason why she so often handled things herself. It was easier than having to worry about whether or not someone else would do it well—or do it at all, for that matter.

Uncle Joseph raised a bushy brow. "And you walked home in this snow, at this hour, all by yourself? It's rather dark outside, Henrietta, and though the streets between here and the church are relatively safe, I hate to think of you slipping and falling in all this ice we've had."

Her lips parted—then pressed shut again. To admit the truth felt perilously close to confessing to something *more* than truth. But lying? That was unthinkable. She tried for the middle ground. "Mr. Baldwin was kind enough to see me home as far as the gate."

Uncle Joseph's brows lifted still further. "Was he indeed? A considerate young man." His voice was calm, but she detected the slightest gleam of interest behind his spectacles.

Henrietta's pulse leapt. "It was nothing more than courtesy," she said quickly, clutching the shawl tighter about her shoulders. "He didn't want me to slip on the ice, that's all. I mean, most men wouldn't want a woman to risk injury. You pointed that out yourself."

"Mm." Uncle Joseph leaned back in his chair, regarding her steadily, as if he saw far more than she wished him to. "All the same, it's good to know there are gentlemen willing to be so attentive."

The implication in his tone was unbearable. Henrietta turned toward the stairs, her composure fraying. "I'd best go upstairs and put my things away."

"Very well, my dear," Uncle Joseph replied, his voice mild again. But she felt his eyes following her as she climbed the steps, each creak of the wood betraying her haste.

Once in her room, she shut the door and leaned against it, her heart still racing. Courtesy, she told herself. Only courtesy.

Yet she could not shake the image of John Baldwin's face in the lamplight, the quiet force in his words. Nor could she forget how, for the first time in years, someone had suggested she need not carry every burden placed upon her.

Was it ridiculous to be so touched by something so simple? Yes. But the truth was, Henrietta had never been looking for romantic gestures. After all, they were just that—weren't they? Gestures. Empty gestures that, at the end of the day, didn't provide any meaningful joy or comfort or ... anything.

But having a task removed from her, almost against her will? And having someone tell her, firmly and without any known ulterior motive, that she was not built for work—but for joy? Especially a man like Mr. Baldwin, who certainly knew and understood the value of good, hard work?

That was a different beast entirely.

Thankfully, Rose appeared to be in the kitchen with Aunt Lydia, so Henrietta was free to set her satchel on the bed and take her hair down.

This has been such a confusing day.

The streets were quiet now, blanketed in the soft hush of freshly fallen snow. John kept his steps deliberate, though the crisp air seemed to encourage a brisker pace, and yet he lingered on each block longer than necessary.

He could not deny it: he had been glad—no, more than glad—to have escorted Miss Miller home. He hadn't let on how happy he was to be walking beside her, even if she was tired and more ready to be home than she was happy to be walking at his side.

He was being a gentleman by doing so, yes. That was the sensible explanation. A gentleman's duty. And yet, as he walked beneath the dim glow of gas lamps, he felt a thrill that had little to do with propriety.

He ought to have chided himself for it. He ought to remind himself that Miss Miller was scarcely his concern beyond the practical matters of the bazaar. And yet, he could not erase the memory of her expression just moments ago—the faint flush to her cheeks, the way her eyes had momentarily softened when he assured her that Huckabee's suggestion was out of bounds.

A wry smile pressed at the corners of his lips, though he quickly smoothed it away. Ridiculous. A man of his age, of his upbringing, should not feel satisfaction at protecting a young woman from an unnecessary task. And yet, he could not escape the truth of it. He had enjoyed it—no, perhaps he had relished it in a way that was unsettlingly new.

He adjusted the collar of his coat and pulled his gloves a little tighter. His thoughts kept returning, insistently, to the moment he had intervened. He had acted instinctively, guided by a quiet and unshakable sense of rightness. How strange it was to feel both pride and a kind of awe at his own action. Pride because it had been the right thing to do; awe because the simplest act—standing up for her—had revealed something new about himself. He hadn't just defended a committee member; he had protected her. The satisfaction of it was something he'd never known.

He let his gaze wander down the street. Lights glimmered in the windows of homes tucked against the snow-laden trees. Children's laughter, muffled but unmistakable, drifted from some distant house. Families gathered. He had seen it all his life, yet tonight it felt different. He felt keenly aware of the absence of certain things in his own life—of warmth, of untroubled laughter, of companionship that did not come with rules or obligations.

He wondered, briefly, if she would notice that stirring as well. That the air between them had shifted in ways subtle and yet undeniable. John let out a slow breath, condensing it into the cold air in a white plume.

He thought of her again and again, walking beside him, shawl drawn close, hair slightly mussed from the wind, cheeks tinged with cold. She had looked so alive, so completely herself, yet burdened by a weight no one else seemed to notice. And he had noticed. That was something, wasn't it? To see her in that way, to understand even a fragment of the relentless demands she placed upon herself?

And then there was the hope he dared not fully entertain: that she might trust him, that she might allow him to step into her crowded world—not to control it, as she feared, but to share it. To make it lighter, just a fraction, just enough so that she could breathe without guilt.

For now, however, he contented himself with the memory of her slight nod, the soft sound of her voice as she had thanked him, and the gentle echo of her presence beside him.

Chapter Fourteen

A few days after escorting Miss Miller home from the planning meeting, he found himself once again in the midst of a flurry of planning. John felt he was starting to spend more time here than at work—but it didn't matter. It wasn't as if everything didn't slow down around Christmas anyway.

Tables were being arranged for another planning and preparing session, stacks of ledgers and ribbons scattered across the long workbenches. John had spent the last few minutes reviewing the final volunteer list when he saw her: Miss Miller, moving gracefully from one table to another, coiffure coming undone, cheeks flushed from exertion.

She looked adorable, and John hoped someone—anyone—had bothered to tell her. Frankly, he wasn't sure the compliment would be welcome from him, so he kept his lips tightly shut.

Of course, Isaiah Huckabee was already there, following her about with that infuriatingly confident ease he seemed to carry everywhere. John noticed, immediately, how Huckabee slid an arm over her shoul-

der as though it belonged there, as though the world ought to rec-
ognize her as his companion. Miss Miller stiffened, stepping sideways, subtly, but Huckabee followed with the same motion, lightly
brushing her arm. The gesture could have passed as friendly—or at
least innocuous—but John's eyes narrowed. He could see the subtle
stiffening of Miss Miller's body.

She didn't want him to touch her. It wasn't invited.

And yet Huckabee continued?

John's stomach twisted. Even if she weren't Miss Miller, the woman
he was so very captivated by, it would be wrong for Huckabee to
continue imposing upon her this way, in a public setting, at a place
where she had much to do and many people to speak to, where she
could not make a scene without drawing the attention of everyone she
respected most.

"Now, we'll need a few men to help move the tables after the
next rehearsal," Isaiah was saying, his tone light but deliberate, loud,
unconcerned with being overheard, as if Miss Miller's approval—and
that of everyone else who would hear his ceaseless interfering with
things he couldn't understand—were automatic. Why was he here
anyway? "And, of course, we'll need someone to organize a cleaning
crew to follow them. Don't worry, Henrietta; I'm sure you can handle
that part yourself."

Miss Miller's hand hovered near a stack of ribbons. She straightened, smiled faintly, and leaned away. "I'll see what I can do," she said, a
slight pause in her voice betraying the hesitation she always used when
trying to redirect Huckabee without outright confrontation.

Did Huckabee not care that she was trying to remove herself from
his presence?

The man laughed, a low, teasing sound that carried easily across
the room. "Oh, come now. You've always been able to handle these

things. You never disappoint, do you?" He let his hand linger just a little longer on her shoulder, his confidence almost mocking in its persistence.

John's chest tightened. He could see the flicker of unease in her eyes, the small tight motion of her hands, the slight tremor in her step as she shifted away from Isaiah yet again. Something inside him snapped—not anger exactly, but a fierce protectiveness. The thought that popped into his mind once again was, "How dare he?"

And honestly, John didn't care if he ever got to talk Miss Miller home again—or even talk to her. Huckabee's behavior was beyond the pale. There was no tolerating it; not if John was a decent man at all, and he liked to flatter himself that he was.

Stepping forward, John kept his tone casual, as if he were merely participating in the conversation, but every word was precise, deliberate. "I think Miss Miller and I should take a look at the layout for the refreshments table," he said. His voice was calm, even, but unmistakable in its clarity. "Miss Miller, will you help me with this, please?"

Huckabee froze mid-laugh, and his eyes narrowed slightly.

That's right, you presumptuous bully. You have a little competition. Can you handle that?

Miss Miller turned to John with a subtle tilt of her head that didn't go unnoticed by Huckabee, if his slightly frustrated pout was anything to go off of. Huckabee, however, didn't seem ready to concede the space just yet. He gave a half-smile, leaning in as though to reclaim the moment. "Oh? I thought—"

"Miss Miller, you've been doing more than enough." John stepped forward. He took an unchristian delight in being slightly taller and broader than Huckabee was, and he filled the space at Miss Miller's side easily enough. He slid into the space she'd vacated as she stepped back once again from her unwanted admirer, placed a hand lightly on the table—not in her space, but certainly in Huckabee's.

Huckabee jerked back as if stung by one of the bows on the table before him.

John smiled and turned to Miss Miller. "Let's go over this together. I'd appreciate your thoughts—you always know best about these things."

Miss Miller let out a small, almost inaudible huff of laughter. "Thank you, Mr. Baldwin. I'm sure that's not true, but I'll do what I can."

Huckabee's eyes flicked between them, and for the first time that morning, John saw a hint of something like unease cross his rival's face. He didn't speak; he just wandered off.

That's right. Give her a little breathing room, why don't you?

The conversation that followed was mundane on the surface: table arrangements, volunteer timing, the placement of extra wreaths for the entryway. Yet John's focus was split; he couldn't help but watch Huckabee watching *them*, approaching them every so often on an unknown errand of some sort, and Miss Miller, subtly shifting to ensure that the physical space between herself and Huckabee remained hers to control.

"I think Booth Five should be closer to the back wall," Miss Miller was saying as Huckabee once again eased closer then backed off. "That way, the children's crafts won't interfere with the foot traffic, and the older volunteers can move more freely without bumping into them."

John nodded, keeping his hand on the edge of the table. "I agree. And we can assign one volunteer to manage the table flow during the peak hours. That way it won't all fall on your shoulders." He let his gaze meet hers for a moment, and she responded with a subtle nod, the faintest smile tugging at her lips.

Huckabee, clearly still trying to assert himself, somehow managed to wiggle his way around to John's other side. What a worm. "Well, if anyone can keep it running smoothly, it's Miss Miller. She's remarkable, you know. Always knows what needs to be done." His tone carried a faint edge, a challenge disguised as praise.

John's voice was calm but direct. "She isn't doing it alone today. That's why I'm helping. It's a team effort." His eyes didn't leave Huckabee's face, steady and unflinching. "And she deserves to have a choice about what she takes on. You don't get to add to her list without asking."

Miss Miller didn't say anything, but her hand brushed against John's accidentally as she reached for a pencil.

Or was it accidental? John wasn't sure. He wished it weren't—but it seemed unlikely that she would have voluntarily chosen to touch him.

Wasn't it?

Huckabee gave a short laugh, a little strained, and shrugged. "All right, all right. You two seem to have it under control." He straightened, but John didn't move. The silent message was clear: this was no longer a free pass for presumptions or casual claims. Miss Miller had someone watching her back—and if he wanted to get around John, he was going to have to gain a little bulk, because he was not going to be moved by anything save physical force—or Miss Miller telling him to leave.

At last, Huckabee strutted off to the other side of the room.

"Thank you," Miss Miller murmured as she scratched away with the pencil she'd collected. "Isaiah means well, but he's not very helpful, I'll admit."

"Just making sure you don't take more than you should," he replied evenly.

"I don't know what to think of you, Mr. Baldwin," she added in the same undertone. "It is clear you don't care for Isaiah."

John swallowed. Did he dare say it? Perhaps now was the time to be bold. "I don't care for any man who makes a woman feel uncomfortable by repeatedly encroaching upon a woman's person and forcing his physical presence on her body. I promise you I would never do such a thing—and so I cannot tolerate it in another person."

Her throat shifted as she seemed to swallow. "That's very noble of you."

"Yes." John hesitated then added, "I do not know that I would have noticed, until recently. But I couldn't help noticing today. I could see you were uncomfortable, and that seemed suddenly unpardonable."

Miss Miller glanced at him then went back to the notebook in front of her.

"I suppose what I'm trying to say," John said in the same undertone, "is I just notice *you*."

"Oh." The word wasn't said in disappointment or derision, though. It was honest, soft surprise. "Is that so?"

"Yes."

And if John were bold, he would have said, "What if we were to discuss this at a later date?" or "May I walk you home after we're done here?" or "Would you be open to me calling on you some day?"

But for now, he simply let the words hang in the air between them. There was time for that. After all, they still had another week or so of bazaar prep, then the bazaar itself.

And honestly, he felt that adding another item to her to-do list right now, regardless of his own selfish wishes, would be wildly unfair.

Yes, he could wait. They had all the time in the world—and getting to know each other more in the meantime couldn't be a bad thing either.

But John was quite sure he was more than a little interested in Henrietta Miller.

Chapter Fifteen

I t was time at last for those final touches that Henrietta stressed over every year to an excess. Always, there was something—the bazaar was a massive endeavor, and even with a larger team, things were often missed.

That said, Henrietta couldn't help but feel Mr. Baldwin's touches as she walked slowly from table to table, rearranging ribbons and straightening boxes and adjusting wreaths. Each task felt a little lighter than usual—not because of the work itself, or because anything had technically become easier, but because of the way the hall seemed to hum with anticipation.

The faint thrill of the last few meetings was practically humming through her as she continued on her endless circuit. She could still feel the light brush of Mr. Baldwin's hand against hers—and the thudding of her heart that the occasion had caused. She could still see Isaiah's frustrated and angered face. And more than that, she had experienced more and more of Mr. Baldwin's attentions lately.

Oh, he wasn't terribly obvious. Little comments about how he'd noticed she was tired. Subtle decisions to take over one of her tasks himself—or find things to take off her plate. He'd even found a way to relegate the children's choir to an older woman who was delighted to spend more time with the adorable little ones—which meant for once in her life, Henrietta wasn't late for adult choir practice herself.

This was especially important since she had a solo this year at one of the bazaar performances which she wanted to go well. She thought she had it perfected—but at the same time, it never hurt to practice more.

A slight creak in the floorboards, and she turned to face the man himself. There was a rare smile on his face as he approached her. A sudden warmth spread through her chest, as it seemed to lately when she saw him.

Or heard his voice. Or thought about him. Or dreamed about him, really. In truth, Henrietta had had better sleep in the last week because of him.

She really was smitten, wasn't she? And even if it was just a temporary infatuation, she was grateful for all he'd done for her.

Her hands grew slightly clumsy, fumbling as she attempted to align a row of ribbons while also gawking at him like a silly schoolgirl. She cursed herself silently. She couldn't look at him too long, she couldn't think about him too deliberately—she had work to do, after all—but every glance pulled her attention back.

He approached with a small paper bag in hand. "Miss Miller," he said, his voice carrying just enough amusement—almost as if he were laughing at himself—to make her pulse quicken.

"Yes?" she asked, trying to keep her voice steady.

He held the bag toward her. "Gingerbread. Consider it a small morale boost for the hardest-working planner I know."

Her fingers brushed his as she took the bag. A jolt shot through her, sharp and delicious, and she caught herself holding the contact a second too long before she drew back, cheeks warm. She couldn't decide if the squirming in her stomach was from the gingerbread, his nearness, or the fact that he touched her.

"You think a cookie will save me?" she asked lightly, forcing a playful tone.

"Perhaps it'll earn me a smile," he said. "That'd be a good reward, I think."

She felt herself smile despite her best efforts.

The corner of his mouth lifted in that little half-smirk that made her heart race and mind stutter.

She accepted the cookie but put it aside for now—she would need to savor it. "What did you come here for? The only people left are those who have last-minute setup before tomorrow." The hall was mostly empty; after they left, so could she, though she wouldn't want to. If Henrietta had her way, she'd stay in the hall all night, guarding her hard work as a dragon guarded its hoard. But that wasn't practical.

"I knew you'd be here," Mr. Baldwin said absently, also turning to one of the booths and inspecting it. "I hope you don't mind me following you around."

That was the other thing—where Isaiah presumed, Mr. Baldwin asked. Deliberately. And Henrietta wished she were bold enough to do what she would never do for Isaiah—tell Mr. Baldwin clearly that she welcomed his attentions.

She could not be so bold, so all she said was, "You're very helpful to me, Mr. Baldwin."

"John." He said his own name somewhat impulsively, she thought; she caught his surprised expression, which then slid into a satisfied firmness. "Would you call me by my given name?"

"I would like that," Henrietta said, "but of course, you must call me

Henrietta."

He took a step toward her, close but not too close, and held out his hand, expression serious, though perhaps mockingly so. "Henrietta."

Laughing, she accepted his hand. "John."

He shook her hand, and Henrietta pretended that having Mr. Baldwin—John—hold her hand in his wasn't a riot of sensations.

"Let me help you with whatever last-minute adjustments you have, then I'll walk you home," John suggested.

"I'd like that."

As they moved side by side through the hall, commenting on decorations and adjusting tablecloths, every touch—brief, accidental, sometimes lingering—sent little sparks up her arms and down her spine. She caught herself leaning slightly toward him, noting the way he adjusted his posture as if aware of her movements, as if he was aware of *her*—as if he was leaning into her, too.

"You're insufferable," she murmured at one point when he managed to touch her hand—again—shaking her head. "I know we're not alone, but we should still be careful. People will talk."

"What would they say?" he said in an undertone, his eyes moving over to a cluster of women by one booth, others by another. "What will they say, when they see how we're behaving?"

She couldn't stop a smile from spreading across her face. "They might say ... that we are always seen together."

"Yes. And?"

"That there's more to that than just ... than just planning a bazaar."

"Yes," John said seriously. "They might say that, too."

"Perhaps they would even say that you are showing a marked interest in me." Henrietta swallowed and forced the next few sentences out: "That you can't possibly have as much reason to linger about me as you do. That perhaps, just perhaps, the way we find ourselves looking at each other and, even, touching each other's hands—even if it's innocent—is ... not nothing. It's not an accident." She took a deep breath and concluded with, "At least, that's what they'll say."

John smiled then, and nodded, and said, "And it would be true. At least, Henrietta, it would be true for me. This is not accidental at all—for me."

Heat scoured her face and neck, and she whirled away from him, needing something grounding. Though the clarity was refreshing and good, it was also overwhelming in the moment. In a much louder voice than was necessary, she said, "Everything's nearly ready for the refreshments." She gestured toward a table stacked with tins of preserves and plates of baked goods. "Do you think we've missed anything?"

"Yes," he replied, his attention snapping back to the task at hand in that way she found endlessly attractive, "but we'll assign someone to manage the table flow during peak hours. That way, it won't all fall on your shoulders. You're far too talented to spend the day exhausted at every task," he added, careful not to be overheard by the others bustling around.

She felt herself blush. "I—thank you," she murmured. "That's what I think I'm enjoying most. Being noticed."

"Henrietta," he murmured, leaning slightly closer as he adjusted the table edge, "I notice you. Always."

Her stomach fluttered. She could hardly find words, but she forced herself to speak—for once, bravely. "I notice you too," she admitted, voice trembling just enough to betray her nerves.

He allowed another of those smirks, just enough to convey satisfaction and delight without breaking his composed demeanor.

"You truly are insufferable," she said again, because he made her breathless and silly, and she had to get back at him somehow for daring to shake her composure and make her feel—feel *everything*.

"Perhaps," he said lightly, "but you seem to enjoy it. You can tell me if you're not."

"No. I am."

They finally finished with their work and managed to hustle everyone else out of the building into the snowy evening. There were enough people leaving at the same time that no one looked askance at them beginning the short walk back to Henrietta's uncle's home together.

The cold air hit her cheeks as they stepped outside, and Henrietta pulled her shawl tighter around her shoulders, though in truth, she barely felt it. Her mind and her heart and her soul were full of John now. John offered her his arm, and she took it. Snow crunched softly beneath their feet, and the streetlamps cast a gentle glow across the frosted sidewalks.

He walked with that calm assurance she had come to notice over the past weeks, but tonight there was something different—a slightly slower step, perhaps, as if he were savoring the moment, and a serious intentionality in his expression, as if he were considering something deeply.

At last, they arrived at her uncle's house. They passed through the gate, up onto the porch, and John turned to her.

"Henrietta," he said quietly, "may I ask you something?"

She looked up, catching the faint glimmer in his eyes. "Of course," she said softly, though her stomach tightened.

He hesitated just a heartbeat, then asked in a low, deliberate tone, "May I kiss you?"

Her breath caught. She had wondered if he might ask her, but hearing the words spoken aloud—so careful, so respectful—made her knees feel weak. "Yes," she said. "You may."

For a moment, he seemed to consider his approach, then he reached for her, his gloved hand lightly cupping her cheek. The cool wool was soft against her face. He leaned forward and brushed his lips against hers, a feather-light touch that made her eyes flutter closed. His lips were warmer than they had any right to be, and softer, and more perfect.

Henrietta's hands trembled slightly—unsure what to do with themselves—as she leaned in, allowing herself to sink into the kiss, feeling the subtle brush of his lips. The world around them seemed to fade: the porch, the sounds of her family beyond the door, even the chill of the evening. Only this—the warmth, the closeness, the undeniable pull between them—remained.

When he finally pulled back enough to let her catch her breath, she opened her eyes to find him watching her with that careful attentiveness that had become so characteristic of him.

"I just thought, after this evening, that I couldn't wait any longer for that," he whispered, slowly lowering his hand and drawing away from her. "Was that all right?"

"Yes," she replied, a little breathlessly. "That was more than all right. That was wonderful."

He reached out, brushing a strand of hair from her face, letting his fingers linger just long enough to make her shiver. "I think we should take this slowly," he said. "But I also think we both know what we want."

She nodded, her heart pounding. "Yes. I think we do."

"We should try to rest tonight," he said in an undertone, "and we should enjoy the bazaar. And then ... and then we'll talk."

"Yes," she agreed. It wouldn't do to try to settle everything tonight. "But you're ...?"

"I'm courting you, Henrietta Miller." He smiled. "And you must know that ... that I wouldn't do that if I weren't very interested. Very interested indeed."

"I'm also very interested," Henrietta confirmed.

He chuckled and nodded. "I should go," he said, but he was reaching for her again. Slowly he leaned in again, letting his lips meet hers once more. This kiss was different—longer, more assured, carrying the weight of unspoken promises and the warmth of mutual desire.

Henrietta's hands found their way to his chest, fingers lightly clutching his coat as she melted into the moment. Each second stretched, allowing them to savor the connection, the closeness, the subtle, intoxicating charge that had been building between them for weeks.

When they finally parted, breathless and grinning like fools, Henrietta felt a dizzying combination of delight and relief.

"Good night, Henrietta," he said softly, his forehead resting briefly against hers before he stepped back. "Sleep well, and know that I'll be thinking of you. I'll see you tomorrow, all right?"

"You too, John," she whispered, her heart full, her spirit light, and a secret thrill bubbling just beneath the surface. "I'll see you then."

She watched him leave, snow crunching beneath his boots, feeling the echo of his kiss linger in the warmth of her cheeks, the racing of her heart, and the gentle joy that had taken root in her chest. Tonight, the world felt slightly different—brighter, lighter, filled with possibility—and she knew, in the quiet certainty of her own heart, that nothing would ever feel quite the same again.

Chapter Sixteen

Henrietta awoke before dawn with a curious flutter in her chest. In truth, she had slept little, tossing and turning in the bed beside Rose, playing over the memory of John's kisses. She felt as if his touch had imprinted itself upon her very soul.

As she rose from the bed, she groaned softly. Her bones ached, her head felt full and heavy, and her throat had a rawness to it—all signs of little sleep. Yet the show must go on, as it always did. She pressed her hands to her heated cheeks as she dressed. She had promised herself not to dwell on it, not to let her heart run wild, but how was she to contain such a thing? To know that Mr. Baldwin—*John*—desired her enough to lean in, to claim what could only be called a stolen kiss, when only a few weeks ago he had been nothing but a stranger?

But he was not a stranger to Henrietta anymore. He was a near and dear friend, and now he had become something more. Though he had not confessed feelings for her, or firmly stated that he wished to marry her, he had come very close to doing just that.

And today they would spend the whole day together, shoulder

to shoulder, in the church's grandest undertaking of the year. He would see her triumph—he would see how much this night meant for everyone, and especially for her.

She tied her bonnet with fingers that trembled and when she shook with a chill, she convinced herself it was the brisk cold of December air seeping through the windows.

But maybe this was what it felt like to be in love.

Though Henrietta was early to the church, she wasn't the first arrival. Already the scent of cinnamon and roasting chestnuts lingered at the doors, drifting from the refreshments stall someone had insisted on setting up outdoors despite the chill. Inside, the fellowship hall and adjoining classrooms had been transformed. Colorful ribbons and garlands hung from the rafters; makeshift booths lined the walls, their tables laden with hand-sewn linens, jars of preserves, toys carved by parishioners, and every manner of baked good imaginable.

Henrietta drew a long breath. It will be a triumph, she told herself. A triumph for the church, for the orphans who would benefit, and perhaps—though she dared not whisper it aloud—for her own battered sense of worth.

"Miss Miller."

Her heart jolted at the low, familiar voice. She turned to find John standing behind her, coat collar dusted with snow, his expression warmer than it had ever been before.

"Henrietta," she reminded him, hoping that the intimacy of the night before hadn't dissipated in the cold light of day.

He nodded. "Henrietta. You're early."

"As are you," she managed, and cursed inwardly the flutter that crept into her tone.

His eyes softened, almost amused. "I thought perhaps I might escort you in. But you've beaten me to it."

She smiled, unable to help herself. His presence—solid, quiet, reassuring—settled something inside her, even as her nerves continued their wild dance.

"Shall we see how everything looks before the rush begins?" he asked.

She nodded, and together they walked among the booths, pausing here and there as women bustled to set out wares and men shifted tables into place. Several stopped John to ask about arrangements for the evening's nativity tableau, and he answered with that calm thoroughness she had come to know so well.

She stole glances at him while he spoke—the way his brow furrowed slightly when considering a problem, the measured cadence of his voice, the way his gloved hand rested lightly at the small of her back to steer her past a stack of crates. That gentle touch sent warmth racing through her, even as she told herself it was nothing. He was simply being courteous.

Still, she could not erase the memory of his lips against hers.

Of course, the peace of the early morning couldn't last. The day passed in a whirl. Henrietta scarcely had time to breathe, let alone sit. She directed volunteers at the baked goods raffle, sorted donations, soothed a squabble between two children over a toy horse, and delivered a missing basket of preserves to its proper booth.

Through it all, John remained near—never hovering, never overbearing, but quietly attentive. Once he appeared at her side with a cup of hot tea.

"You've not stopped since sunrise," he said mildly, handing it to her.

"Neither have you." She took a sip and smiled over the rim. "But thank you."

"Will you sit a moment?"

"There's no time." She gestured to the bustle around them.

"There's always something to do, as well you know. I'll sleep well tonight—but there'll be no stopping until then."

His eyes lingered on her a moment longer, as if he wished to argue. But he only inclined his head and moved off to help Mrs. Baldwin hang the last of the nativity backdrop.

Henrietta drained the tea and set the cup aside, determined to ignore the ache in her throat and the heaviness in her limbs. Perhaps it was only weariness. She would push through.

By midday the crowd poured in—a stream of parishioners, neighbors, and curious passersby eager for an afternoon of festivity. The air grew thick with laughter, with the clink of coins, with the mingled aromas of fresh bread and pine.

Henrietta darted from booth to booth, answering questions, tallying raffle entries, ensuring the children in the choir had found their places for the evening. Every so often she felt John's gaze across the room, steady upon her, and the knowledge both steadied and unsettled her.

But her throat ached more sharply now, and a faint pounding had begun at her temples. The noise, the strain of the crowd, the long day—that was all; it was fine. She would endure.

When she paused to catch her breath near the refreshment stall, John appeared once more, this time with a plate in hand.

"You've not eaten," he said.

She blinked. "I haven't had a moment—"

"Then take one now." He pressed the plate into her hands—gingerbread, still warm, dusted with sugar.

Her lips parted in protest, but his eyes held hers with such quiet insistence that she laughed softly, the sound half a surrender. "Very well. But only because you look so determined."

"Determination is one of my faults, I'm told."

"One of your strengths, I should think," she said, breaking off a piece of gingerbread. The sweetness melted on her tongue, and suddenly she realized how hollow her stomach had felt.

John watched her with an expression she could not quite decipher—something gentle, almost protective, but with an intensity beneath it that made her pulse quicken.

"You see?" he said quietly. "Not everything must rest on your shoulders. Allow someone else the chance to carry a part."

Her smile faltered, for the words struck deep. She forced a light tone. "If I stopped, the whole affair might collapse."

"Or it might not," he murmured. "The world does not end when Henrietta Miller rests."

She looked away, heart thudding, and made a jest of it. "I shall have to test that theory another time."

But inside, some part of her trembled. And it wasn't just the persistent chill and the shaking of her hands.

The afternoon stretched long. The children's skits drew laughter, the raffle prizes caused excitement, and the stalls grew lighter as the funds for the orphan charity swelled. Henrietta told herself she ought to rejoice, but her body grew heavier with each hour. Her throat burned now, her head ached fiercely, and more than once she swayed where she stood.

John saw it. She knew he did. Once she caught his frown across the room, and another time he touched her elbow as she brushed past, murmuring, "Sit. Please. Just for a few minutes, Henrietta."

She only shook her head and pressed on.

For she could not falter. Not today, with the bazaar—not tonight, when her choir solo awaited. Not when she might yet prove—to herself, to the congregation, perhaps even to John—that she was capable of giving something beautiful, something worthy.

As dusk fell and the final lamps were lit, Henrietta stood with the choir in the side chamber, waiting to take their places. Her heart pounded not only with nerves but with the edges of what might very well be a fever. She knew it now; the heat in her cheeks, the ache in her bones. She should have admitted it hours ago.

She closed her eyes a moment, breathing in the scent of melting wax and evergreen bows, and whispered a prayer. *Let me be able to sing. Let me hold myself together, just one more moment, without failing.*

When she opened her eyes, John was there in the aisle, directing the children into place. For an instant, their gazes met. His expression was steady, grounding, as if to say: *You are not alone.*

And her heart, for all its pounding, lifted. She would not fail—surely not. She had done so much before; she only needed to hold it together for another half hour, and then, John was right—she must sit down.

But not yet.

The sanctuary was hushed now. Candles glowed in every window, but their flames wavered and doubled in her vision, smearing against panes rimed with frost. The air was thick—too thick—with pine and beeswax, cloying on her tongue, and even the faint sweetness of sugared nuts from the refreshment stall outside made her stomach turn. Families filled the pews in a restless blur, children's movements rustling louder than they ought, scraping at her temples.

Henrietta stood at the edge of the choir loft, hands clenched tight against her skirts. Her throat burned. The ache in her head throbbed in rhythm with her pulse. The children had just finished their carol, their voices thin and far away, as though carried from another room. The ripple of applause that followed reached her only dimly, muffled and slow, as if she were underwater. Next would come the adult choir—two familiar hymns sung in harmony. Then her solo.

O Holy Night. It was a beautiful carol, but a challenging one—but surely she was up for the task. She pressed her chapped lips together, forcing a slow breath. She had sung it a dozen times in rehearsal. She knew each rise and fall, every measure. But tonight it felt like a mountain too steep for her faltering strength.

Still—she must. She could not falter now, not after all the labor of the day. Not with John there. He would be listening. Would the words he spoke if she failed be "I told you so"? She didn't believe that, but the very thought brought half a sob to her throat. She reminded herself that when she was unwell, she felt extra emotional, but it wasn't just him—the whole congregation would be listening.

She must sing.

The choir began. Henrietta lifted her voice with the others, grateful for the strength of many surrounding her own. She could blend, let her rawness hide beneath their fuller tones. For a few precious moments she felt steadied.

Then came the final chord. Silence fell again, weighty and expectant.

My cue.

Henrietta stepped forward. A wave of dizziness swept over her; she blinked hard, forcing her vision to focus. Were those black spots before her eyes? It didn't matter. She could sing.

Mrs. Baldwin gave her a nod from the front pew, face bright with anticipation. Somewhere in the second row Henrietta caught sight of Rose, wide-eyed, hands clasped. And beyond them—John. Standing near the side aisle, his arms folded, expression unreadable in the half-light but his gaze fixed wholly upon her.

He looked ... concerned.

That was odd. She was doing just fine.

She drew in breath. The opening notes floated from the small organ.

"'O holy night, the stars are brightly shining—'"

Her voice wavered. She pressed forward, willing it stronger.

"'It is the night of our dear Savior's birth—'"

The notes caught in her throat. A rasp tore through the sound, cracking it in two. She swallowed hard, tried again.

"'Long lay the world—'"

But nothing came. Only a strangled whisper, hoarse and broken.

A murmur rippled through the pews. Somewhere a child giggled before being hushed. Henrietta's vision swam. Her throat constricted as if clamped shut.

She tried again, forcing air upward, but the sound came raw and pitiful. The words disintegrated into coughs.

No—no, no, no.

Heat surged in her cheeks. The candle flames blurred. Her hands trembled so violently she clasped them behind her back to hide it, but the effort only unbalanced her further.

She could not go on.

The organ faltered, chords stumbling to a stop. The silence that followed was merciless.

Henrietta stood frozen, shame roaring in her ears. This was worse than every whispered fear, worse than every warning her body had given her. She had failed—before God, before the congregation, before *John*.

Her breath hitched. With a desperate sob, she turned and fled from the loft, skirts swishing against the steps as she stumbled into the side corridor.

The hallway was dim, lined with cloaks left on pegs, the muffled sound of the crowd behind her. Henrietta pressed her back against the wall, gulping for breath. Her throat ached, her chest heaved, but it was nothing compared to the tearing inside her.

She slid down the plaster until she sat on the floor, pressing her hands over her face. A sob escaped, jagged and uncontainable. Another followed. She tried to stifle the sound, ashamed, but the more she fought, the harder they came.

All her striving—all her endless labor, her desperate grasping for worth—had come to this. Public failure. Humiliation. Confirmation that she was, indeed, weak and unfit. She couldn't hold it all together. She couldn't do everything. She couldn't—

"Henrietta."

She startled. The voice was low, smooth, too close. When she lifted her head, Isaiah stood in the corridor.

Before she could scramble to her feet, he was kneeling beside her. "My poor girl."

She shook her head, choking out, "Please—"

But he didn't wait. He reached for her hands, pried them gently from her face, and drew her against his chest. "You mustn't cry so. It's nothing. A trifle. It doesn't matter. Everyone will forget by morning. Everyone can see that you're not well."

She stiffened, her hands pushing weakly at his shoulders. She didn't want this. "Isaiah—don't—"

He hushed her, brushing a hand against her hair. His other arm wrapped firmly around her back, holding her as though she were a child.

Henrietta's breath came shallow, panic rising. She tried again to pull free, but his hold only tightened.

"You're overwrought," he murmured. "You need someone to care for you. I will. I promise you, I will." Before she could speak, he bent and pressed a kiss to her brow.

Her stomach lurched. She shoved against him with all the strength she could muster. But her protest came too late.

A sound at the corridor's end—a sharp intake of breath.

Henrietta twisted, eyes widening.

John stood there.

For one shattering instant their gazes met. His face was stricken, pale, hurt. His mouth opened, as if to speak—but no words came. Then he turned. His shoulders stiffened, and he walked swiftly back the way he had come.

"No—" Henrietta cried, surging to her feet. "John, wait—"

But Isaiah caught her arm. "Let him go," he said firmly.

She whirled on him, fury and anguish colliding. "Release me!"

His grip tightened. "You'll only make a scene. It's better this way."

Her heart pounded. She yanked, twisted, but his hand held fast. By the time she wrenched herself free, the corridor was empty. John was gone.

Gone.

The word echoed through her, hollow and final.

She staggered back against the wall, pressing her hand to her burning forehead. Tears blurred her vision, hot and unrelenting.

Not only had she failed, but the one man whose regard she treasured most now believed her false, faithless—willing in another's arms.

And it was her own weakness that had brought it to pass.

The rest of the evening blurred. Isaiah brought her to her cousin with little further protest—at least, he didn't try to press further advantage. Henrietta scarcely knew what words she muttered to Rose, what platitudes she gave the committee members about being "unwell." Her body ached, her fever climbed, and Rose brought her home. At last she could collapse into bed, where she buried her face in the pillow and wept until no tears remained.

John's face haunted her—the look of devastation, the swift retreat.

The closing off of all that had begun to blossom between them.

The memory of Isaiah's hold made her skin crawl. She scrubbed her forehead with the sleeve of her nightgown as though she could erase the unwelcome kiss.

But she could not erase the truth: John believed what he had seen, and she had no strength left to prove otherwise.

The darkness pressed close.

Henrietta felt utterly alone.

Chapter Seventeen

The scene replayed endlessly in his mind.

Henrietta, crumpled in Isaiah's arms. Her tear-streaked face pressed against his shoulder. Isaiah's hand gentle in her hair, his lips brushing her brow.

It had been plain. Intimate. *Undeniable.*

John pushed through the milling crowd in the fellowship hall, offering smiles where required, hearing little of the words spoken to him. The laughter of neighbors, the congratulations for a "successful bazaar," the voices of children begging for more ginger cakes—all of it blurred into meaningless noise.

He had thought—foolishly, it seemed—that Henrietta's glances, her laughter, the warmth of her hand in his, had meant something. That their kisses on her uncle's porch had been the beginning of an understanding. To him, kissing a woman meant commitment. *Serious* commitment. It meant marriage, and soon. It was an unmistakable sign, he'd thought. He wouldn't have kissed her if he wasn't sure of her—and he had been certain she felt the same.

But she had turned so easily into another's embrace.

Not merely another's. *Isaiah's.*

The sight had landed like a blow to the chest. He had felt stripped of breath, as though the air itself had betrayed him. He had fled the corridor before the sound of Henrietta's cry—his name, he thought dimly—could reach him. He hadn't feared for her safety, when the entirety of the choir was within earshot, not to mention the rest of the church beyond—and that had been the only thing that had prompted a moment of hesitation in him before he had run.

And now he could not bring himself to turn back.

"John! *Johnny.* Could you carry this basket to the vestry?" Mother pressed a load of unsold trinkets into his hands before he could protest.

He nodded mutely, bearing the burden away. The motions of labor steadied him, however hollow. In the vestry he set the basket on the long table, then braced his palms against the wood, shoulders hunched.

He'd spent so much time here with Henrietta. In fact, he'd spent so much time everywhere with Henrietta. And he'd thought he'd known her. He'd thought.

He had been deceived.

Or worse—he had deceived himself.

What had ever made him think that Henrietta Miller—bright, graceful, admired by all—would choose him? She might laugh at his dry remarks, might share her burdens freely, but that was pity, perhaps. Gratitude. Not love.

She deserved someone confident, charming, unhesitating. Someone like Isaiah.

John's fists clenched. He loathed the man—his polished gallantry, his smooth words, the proprietary way he had spoken of Henrietta in committee meetings. Yet she had not pushed him away. If she had pushed him toward more propriety at times, that was only natural—any woman might remind her sweetheart of their public setting when he grew too familiar. She was setting boundaries with a man she still admired and enjoyed the presence of—not trying to brush off an unwelcome suitor, as John had assumed. If she had been doing that, she would have made it clear, and Isaiah wouldn't have run to her when she was suffering.

The evening wore on. He made himself useful—stacking chairs, extinguishing candles, guiding half-frozen families to their sleighs. He answered congratulations with murmured acknowledgments.

All the while, he avoided the one place he most ached—and most dreaded—to go.

Henrietta's absence was noted. Rose explained to a few concerned ladies that her cousin was unwell, that she had been carried home to rest. John heard this in passing, heart twisting. *Unwell.* Yes. He had seen the feverish flush in her cheeks. He had worried for her, urged her to rest earlier in the day. She had smiled at him, promised she was fine.

And then she had gone to Isaiah for comfort.

The thought soured even his concern.

By the time the last carriage rattled down the street and the church stood mostly dark, John's body ached with weariness. He gathered his coat and hat and made for the door.

Outside, the night air was sharp, bracing. His breath rose white before him. The snow beneath his boots crunched loud in the stillness.

He longed for solitude. For escape. For the quiet of his own room where he might strip away this humiliating hope that had built inside him, brick by fragile brick, only to be toppled in a single instant.

How foolish he had been.

A man of his years, allowing himself to dream like a lovesick boy.

Henrietta had been kind. Too kind. He had mistaken it for something more—had perhaps even pressed his advantage on her uncle's porch, as only a cad would do.

He pressed a hand to his brow, willing the ache away. He must forget the touch of her hand, the warmth of her smile, the caress of her lips. He must forget the way she had looked at him on that walk home from the church, when he had dared to hope she might see something in him worth cherishing.

The sooner he put such thoughts aside, the better.

For her sake—and for his own.

Chapter Eighteen

Henrietta surfaced into consciousness slowly, as if her body clung to sleep the way a drowning person clutched at a floating board. The room around her swam in and out of focus—the dim flicker of a fire in the grate, the familiar outlines of the bedroom she shared with Rose, the faint creak of the rocking chair where her cousin sat with her sewing.

Her throat ached, and her head throbbed with a dull, pounding weight. Even the touch of the blankets against her skin felt heavy, oppressive, though chills still shivered through her. She shifted, and the movement startled Rose into glancing up.

"You're awake," Rose whispered, abandoning her mending to perch on the edge of the bed. Her face, always so quick to express amusement, was drawn and worried. "How do you feel?"

Henrietta swallowed—or tried to. The effort burned. Her voice rasped like a file against stone. "Like a barn owl in winter."

Rose blinked, then smiled faintly. "You poor goose. That's no answer at all." She tucked the covers higher beneath Henrietta's chin, her hands gentle but brisk.

Memory returned then, unbidden, dragging Henrietta down into the pit she had tried not to fall into even in her fever dreams. The crowded church sanctuary. The children's carol ending. The silence as she stepped forward for her solo. The first trembling note that had cracked, split, and died in her throat.

Her humiliation washed over her again, so sharp she felt her face burn even through the fever. She had fled—oh, what a coward she had been! She had run like a child from the stage, leaving the choir and the congregation to stare after her. And then—

Henrietta squeezed her eyes shut. *No.* She could not think of it. Not Isaiah's arms around her, not the press of his cheek near her temple, not his murmur of consolation. Certainly not the moment when she had looked up and seen John in the archway, his face stricken—before he turned and strode away without a word.

Her stomach twisted, a knot of misery and shame.

"Henrietta?" Rose's hand brushed her brow, pushing damp curls from her temple. "You're flushed. I'll fetch more cool cloths."

"Don't," Henrietta croaked, catching her wrist weakly. "Stay."

Rose sat again, brows pulled tight together. "You're very ill. It's only a fever, so we needn't worry too much, but Mother's been beside herself. I had to physically block the doorway to keep her from fussing over you all night. She just wants you well. We all do. So you need to rest."

Rest. As if rest could mend the gaping wound in her pride, or the aching loss she felt at John's retreating figure. Henrietta turned her face into the pillow, the linen warm and damp beneath her cheek.

"I've ruined everything," she whispered.

"No," Rose said firmly. "You only fell ill. That is all."

Henrietta shook her head, though the motion made her dizzy. "You didn't see him. John—Mr. Baldwin. He ... he looked at me as though I had betrayed him." Her voice cracked, more from anguish than sickness. "And I didn't, Rose, I swear I didn't—but Isaiah—he—"

Her cousin stiffened. "What did Isaiah do?"

Henrietta pressed her eyes shut, shame prickling across her skin. "He—he embraced me. Without asking. And before I could push him away, John saw. He thought ... he *must* have thought ... That I don't want him. But I do."

There. The words were spoken, and the weight of them made her chest constrict.

Rose's silence stretched a long moment, then she exhaled. Her voice was tight and slightly too loud; there was raw fury tangled in every one of her words. "That man has no business touching you. *None.* If Mr. Baldwin has any sense at all, he will know you did not invite it."

Henrietta laughed bitterly, though it turned into a cough that rattled her chest. "But he does not know, does he? He left. He left me there with Isaiah—and he did not return."

The memory of that abandonment hurt worse than the fever. She had thought—*oh, foolish, foolish heart!*—she had thought John cared for her, that his attentions and gentle teasing, the way he had sought her out, the memory of his lips against hers on the porch—meant something. More than something.

Now it seemed it had all been a fragile illusion.

She bit her lip until she tasted blood. Tears pressed hot against her eyes, but she refused to let them fall. Fever or no fever, she would not cry like a lovesick girl.

Rose touched her shoulder, gently. "Henrietta, perhaps—perhaps you should let him explain. Or at least wait until you are well enough to hear what he has to say."

Henrietta turned toward her, her voice breaking. "What if he never comes? What if he truly believes I—I welcomed it?"

The horror of that possibility left her hollow. If John could think her so reckless, so careless with her affections, then he had never truly known her. And if that was the case, had she ever truly known him?

Rose frowned, but said nothing.

The fire snapped in the grate, and outside the muffled clatter of carriage wheels passed along the cobblestones. Henrietta lay still, her heart aching with every beat, her frame shivering with fever though her cheeks burned.

She thought of John's steady hands, the way he had always seemed to notice when she needed rest, when she pushed herself too far. He had tried to slow her down even that very morning. And she—so eager to prove herself useful—had pushed him away, assuring him she could manage. She had managed herself right into disaster.

Now he was gone, and she couldn't even tell him the truth.

The weight of that thought pressed down on her until she could hardly breathe.

Rose rose at last to fetch water, leaving Henrietta alone with her misery. The minutes stretched, blurred by fever and exhaustion, until she sank back into restless sleep.

But even there, in her dreams, she saw John's face—injured, disbelieving—turning from her in the candlelit hallway.

And she could not call him back.

Chapter Nineteen

J ohn adjusted the stacks of correspondence on his father's desk, sliding each into neat piles with more force than necessary. The harbor outside, visible over the rooftops of Franklin Street, glimmered under a winter sun that offered little warmth.

Normally, the clatter of clerks and boots marked the start of Monday's rhythm, but today each sound only reminded him of the bazaar—the chairs, the organ, Henrietta's faltering voice, Isaiah's hand in her hair. He paused mid-motion, chest tight, unsure whether to keep working or give in to the turmoil thrumming through him.

Dad entered from the adjoining room, a folder tucked under one arm, but he paused when he saw John and raised an eyebrow. "Please tell me you're not mourning another ship gone down. You look like a sad, droopy old hound."

John rolled his eyes. "As far as I know, all ships are safely at harbor."

"Good." Dad circled the desk and collapsed heavily in the custom-built chair he'd had created for his rather large frame. "Go on, son—tell me."

John frowned. He didn't like how insightful Dad could be some-times—how he always knew when something was bothering him. "Am I not allowed some privacy?"

"If you want personal space, stop working at a family business." Dad leaned against the desk. "I assume this has something to do with a certain Miss Miller, though I can't imagine what. She's well, isn't she? Everyone said it was just a fever. You haven't heard anything else, have you?"

John shook his head. "I've heard nothing else." He released a slight, humorless laugh. "It's only—we ... That is, Miss Miller isn't anything to me. Not anymore. I had hoped—but it's not the case."

Dad's brow lifted. "Go on. Sit and talk."

Yet still, John fidgeted. "You know, employers are not supposed to pry into their employees' lives."

"Unfortunately, you're the boss's son; prying is my prerogative. Tell me."

John slumped into the leather chair, fingers twisting in his lap. "You saw that she was not well enough to perform her solo in the choir. It meant a lot to her, but I should have stopped her, perhaps. She was weak—feverish. I saw her flee from the choir loft and followed her, only to see Isaiah Huckabee—He held her. Kissed her. And I ..." His voice faltered. "I left. I knew then that I was wrong; there was nothing between us. Obviously, she wanted *him*. She chose *him* over *me*. I just can't understand how everything between us—our laughter, our talks, our ... our *everything*—meant nothing."

Dad straightened in his seat. "We'll circle back around to your 'everything,' though I've an idea of what that particular euphemism means. But you still think that now? After you walked away and didn't give her the chance to explain herself in the first place?"

John hesitated. It was true that refusing to hear an explanation from her was unwise. That was the sort of thing that led to tragic misunder-standings in terrible dime novels. "I saw what I saw. I can't—*couldn't* believe she would ... But I can't believe she would allow what she allowed with Huckabee unless she were truly interested in pursuing a relationship with him—and not with me." At least, that was what John had understood. Could he have been wrong?

Dad leaned back against the desk, arms crossed. "Johnny, I was at the bazaar. I saw you with her all day. You doted on her, made sure she wasn't overwhelmed, helped with everything. And yet you still believe she's with Isaiah? Because of one private moment you misinterpreted?"

John's jaw tightened. "I saw them. What was I to think, really? She could have pushed him away or told him to back off, but surely I couldn't have misinterpreted a deliberate embrace." At least, it was easier to believe that. "Perhaps she wants him. I had every reason to believe that I was mistaken in thinking she even liked me to begin with. That she ..." He swallowed hard. "That she had no reason to feel anything for me."

"Johnny!" John's eyes flew up to his father's face; his eyes were flashing with a subtle but still apparent anger. "'Reason?' What do you know of 'reason'? Son, listen to me. That 'reason' is nothing but your pride and imagination. The poor girl could barely stand with a fever! Do you have any idea how weak she must have been? And you ran off instead of helping her?"

John's shoulders straightened. It wasn't as simple as that. "I—I thought I was protecting her from me. From my presumption. From embarrassment. She plainly didn't want to see me—"

"What makes you think so?" Dad leaned forward, placing both hands firmly on the desk. "You say you were protecting her, but you know what I think you were doing? You were protecting yourself—and possibly leaving her with someone who would not only fail to protect her himself, but who might possibly have harmed her. No, I don't think it came to that—but Johnny, you can't leave a vulnerable woman alone in a dark hallway with a man who she doesn't appreciate the attentions of! That's the antithesis of chivalry, and yet, that is exactly what you did. You left her exposed because you assumed the worst—left her in the arms of a man who had no right to press himself so. And all because you convinced yourself she wanted it. Do you understand how foolish that looks?"

John recalled the moment in the corridor. Her hands pressed to her face. Her arms barely resting on Huckabee's. She was sick, yes—too sick to react to a man's unwanted advances as she might normally have? He had ignored that. *Could I have been so blind?*

Dad's voice softened slightly, though it remained firm. "You made a disastrous mistake, John. But here's the truth: she didn't want Huckabee. She couldn't have possibly invited him in that moment. If she was too ill to sing, or even to stand in the choir loft, she was too ill to speak or act with clarity. You—" He leaned closer, eyes locked on John's. "You left her to fend for herself while sick and vulnerable. And why? Because you couldn't trust your own judgment? Or because you couldn't let yourself trust her?"

John shook his head, frustration and shame mingling. "I saw it with my own eyes, Dad. I couldn't believe—"

"You assumed what you wanted to see rather than what was actually happening. That's not love, son. That's ego. And worse, it left her open to attention she didn't ask for, from a man you yourself despise."

John twisted a pen in his fingers, watching the harbor's sun glance off the water, trying to shake the image from his mind. Henrietta—feverish, flushed, trembling—pressed against Isaiah's chest.

In the quiet of his father's office, he replayed it differently.

She hadn't looked at Isaiah with desire—she had looked small, weak, frightened. Her arms had barely rested against his as if she were clinging for balance. Could he have been wrong? Could he have misread every glance, every laugh, every hand he had held? His stomach knotted. He had left her there ... exposed ... when all she needed was help.

John's stomach twisted. "I—I never thought of it that way. I thought I was being cautious and respectful. But if what you say is true, then yes, I abandoned her. I left her vulnerable."

Dad's expression softened, hand resting on John's shoulder. "Yes. You did. And now you know. That's the point. You learn from it. She's still that girl you care for, sick and alone, and you have a responsibility to act—sensibly, kindly, and without presumption. Do you understand?"

John nodded slowly. "I do. But it's not any better for me if she didn't want his attentions. After all, if I left her, when she needed me most, she can't possibly want me back."

Dad fixed John with a long look. "Johnny, you'll never know until you try. Temper your actions with patience. She's still recovering—and it may be some time until she could even bring herself to see you, if she was hurt. Send a note, or a small gift. Admit your mistake, beg forgiveness—it never hurts to throw yourself at a woman's feet and beg for unwarranted mercy. Then wait—impatient as you may be—for her to respond."

John leaned back, drawing in a deep breath, the shame still heavy but now mingled with determination—a feeling he was much more comfortable with. "Yes. I'll write her a note and drop it off myself. If I explain that I misread everything, ask for her forgiveness, and promise to see her as soon as she is well—I can at least know I did all I could."

Dad gave a small nod, satisfied. "Good. And remember this, John:

care for her, yes, but never presume. You nearly let your pride cost her more than embarrassment. Learn that lesson, and don't repeat it. I can't promise she'll forgive you, but it's still the right thing to do."

John rose, fingers trembling slightly, quill in hand as he gathered paper. "For the record, 'everything' was two kisses on her uncle's porch. Nothing more. And I had fully planned to make my intentions clear yesterday."

Dad laughed. "Yes, I suspected that might be about the extent of your 'everything.' Go on, son—write that note. See if you can't get your girl back."

John bit back a protest—because after all, wasn't that exactly what he hoped? That Henrietta Miller would become 'his girl'?

Chapter Twenty

The morning sun had only just begun to lift over the rooftops of Philadelphia when a soft knock at the door drew Henrietta from a drowsy half-sleep. She stirred under her blankets, the ache in her throat reminding her she was still far from well, though her fever had faded late last night.

"Henrietta?" It was Rose, bearing a small parcel carefully balanced in her hands. "Your John Baldwin called this morning, left it with instructions to deliver it right away. Are you well enough to see it?"

Henrietta blinked, forcing her limbs to obey enough to sit upright. Her body protested—her bones ached—but curiosity pushed her forward. Rose handed her the parcel.

"Should I sit with you as you open it?" she asked.

Henrietta hesitated then shook her head. "I'd rather open it alone, if that's all right with you, Rose. I'll show you later."

"I understand." Rose smiled and gently pressed Henrietta's shoulder before she left. "Don't become too excited—you really must rest."

After Rose had left the bedroom, and the door clicked shut behind her, Henrietta's fingers trembled as she tore the brown paper wrapping. Inside, neatly arranged, was a small posy of winter flowers: sprigs of holly dotted with red berries, a few delicate violets pressed amid their green, and a faint, sweet scent of hyacinth that made her chest lift just slightly.

Nestled beside the posy was a slender envelope, sealed with a neat wax stamp. And tucked underneath the flowers, she noticed a tiny trinket—a hand-painted porcelain charm in the shape of a dove, its wings lifted as if caught in a breeze.

Her pulse quickened. She unfolded the envelope, revealing John's neat script. Even in writing, he was practical and precise as always, but the gift said much about his interest in her.

Could it be that he wasn't uninterested in her now? That he did understand the interaction with Isaiah for what it was—an ill-fated coincidence, attentions she hadn't wanted or reciprocated?

Miss Miller,

I hope this finds you resting as you ought. I write not because I believe I am deserving of your friendship, but to apologize for my absence at the close of the bazaar. I misread what I saw, and I left you vulnerable when I ought to have acted differently. For that, I am sincerely sorry. I hope no harm has befallen you and that you are recovering well from your illness.

I have sent a small gift, merely to remind you that I am thinking of you, and to offer comfort during your recovery. I do not presume your forgiveness, nor do I presume your company, but I hope that when you are well enough, you might allow me the honor of visiting when you are ready.

Until then, rest well. You have my admiration, always, and my deepest hope that you are cared for as you deserve.

Sincerely,
John Baldwin

Henrietta's hands lingered over the letter. She read it once, then again, slower this time, tasting each carefully chosen word. Every line carried the calm steadiness she had come to associate with him—the thoughtfulness, the attentiveness, the respect. She could almost hear his voice, measured and certain, reminding her that she was seen and valued.

Her gaze fell to the little dove, its tiny wings catching the soft morning light. She ran a fingertip across its surface. Such care had been taken, as it always was with him. The simplest charm, yet she could feel the thought behind it, the intention to bring comfort without presumption. Her chest warmed despite the fever, and a small, almost shy smile lifted her lips.

She leaned back against her pillows, pressing the letter and the trinket to her chest. For a long moment, she allowed herself to feel—hope, relief, a gentle stirring of trust she had feared lost. She had been angry at herself, at John, at the unfairness of the bazaar night. And yet, here he was: careful, sincere, attentive even from a distance, acknowledging his error, and leaving the choice entirely to her.

Her mind, still fogged with the remains of the fever and exhaustion, wandered back over their moments together—the quiet conversations, the stolen glances, the small kindnesses he had offered that day. She thought of the day's chaos, the mishap of her faltering voice, the unwanted attentions of Isaiah, and she realized: John had not only seen her struggles, he had acted, now, in a way that truly protected her dignity and honored her independence.

Tears prickled her eyes, not of shame or frustration this time, but of gratitude and something softer, more tender, that had been suppressed under the weight of recent events. She pressed the letter closer, inhaling the mingled scent of paper, wax, and flowers, and felt a cautious, fragile hope take root.

Perhaps, when she was well, she would see him. Perhaps then she would be able to thank him, not only for his words and gifts but for the care that had quietly bridged the chasm of the bazaar night. For now, it was enough to know that he had acted with thoughtfulness, that he had acknowledged the moment's mistakes, and that he waited—not with impatience, nor with expectation, but with kind constancy and almost businesslike esteem. She understood what a gift that was—that he did not give his respect easily.

The illness would pass. The ache would fade. And when it did, she would know that John Baldwin had not abandoned her—not truly, not ever.

For the first time since that terrible night, she allowed herself to believe that what had been broken might yet be mended.

Chapter Twenty-One

I t had been nearly two weeks since John had sent the note, and every day had been a study in waiting. His work no longer soothed him; the shame of having misjudged her lingered, but beneath it was a growing determination to make amends.

The opportunity arrived this evening at a small holiday gathering hosted by the church's social committee—a festivity meant for the congregation and townsfolk alike, with carols, candlelight, and the aroma of roasted chestnuts and warm cider drifting through the hall. He had arrived early, standing quietly near the doorway, taking in the familiar scene of seasonal decorations, smiling families, and the soft hum of music, when he saw her.

Henrietta stood near a window, framed by the glow of candles. She was watching a group of children chase each other around the hall with a smile on her face—almost a laugh, actually. She looked ... well, restored. At ease. Joyful. And for the first time in weeks, John felt the tight coil of worry in his chest ease, replaced by a surge of anticipation.

He stepped forward, careful not to startle her, hands clasped behind his back. "Miss Miller," he began, voice low, almost reverent. "You look ... well. I'm so glad to see you're recovering. The bazaar was a great success, by all accounts. I was happy to be a small part of it."

Henrietta turned, and he noted the ease in her posture, the lack of tension he had seen the night of the bazaar—and, for that matter, for the entire month prior. "It was," she said, voice light. "But I thought it best I not overextend myself in my recovery, so I asked the other ladies on the various committees to replace me."

John blinked, startled. "Really? I imagine it took an army."

"It did," she admitted, the corners of her lips lifting further. "Five people are doing the work I had intended to. But I needed to do that. At least until the New Year, I've committed to not taking on any additional responsibilities. I'm just going to rest—and experience the joy of Christmas. No one minded, really—or at least, no one who matters minded. For the first time, I'm letting myself simply enjoy the season, without the weight of obligation." She paused, a flicker of something more serious in her eyes. "That includes other sorts of obligations, too. Mr. Huckabee approached me the other day. I believe I made it quite clear that my time and attention are my own to give. I don't believe he will be a bother again."

He nodded slowly, letting her words percolate about in his mind. He had expected that would be the case with Huckabee—he was thankful the man wouldn't impose on her again. And then, a quiet but quick rush of realization hit him—she had changed. She was doing as he had always known she must—and not forced by illness or duty, but by her own choice.

"You're ... making yourself rest," he said, the statement more of a marvel than a question.

"Yes," she said, hesitating, then adding thoughtfully, "I know when the New Year comes, I will be tempted to add more things to my to-do list than any one person could reasonably be asked to do. So I was considering—what might help me ensure that doesn't happen again. What if I were to have an assistant?"

"An assistant?" His brow furrowed slightly, unsure where this was heading.

"Yes. Someone I see every day, who would be willing to discuss my duties with me—and gently point me toward rest. Perhaps even firmly state that I am not to commit myself to more than I can handle."

John's heart gave a quiet, amused lift. "Ah. I suppose that would be ... useful. But—"

"Sometimes," she said, tilting her head just so, a playful glint in her eyes, "I think you might need something similar, Mr. Baldwin."

He froze for a heartbeat. "What do you mean?"

"I am told you are a single-minded man when it comes to your career," she said, voice gentle, "but work is not everything, is it?"

He inclined his head, slow and deliberate. "Indeed, it is not."

"Which leads me to this conclusion," she said, stepping slightly closer. "We both need an assistant—a live-in help, if you will; someone to offer firm but gentle accountability. Someone who might lovingly guide us to be the best version of ourselves."

John's pulse quickened as understanding dawned. A smile tugged at his lips. "Oh." He swallowed. "I ... I see what you mean."

"I just think it's interesting," she said lightly, though her eyes lingered on him, "that we both share the same need."

John's chest tightened, and he leaned closer, catching the subtle invitation hidden beneath her words. "Then may I—may I be that for you? I would gladly court you, if you would allow it."

Her smile deepened, laughter soft but not shy. "I think," she said, voice warm, "that would be quite agreeable. But only if you truly accept the other half of this arrangement—you must allow me to remind *you* when you overextend yourself."

"I think I could manage that," he said, and in that simple exchange, a mutual understanding—and a shared promise—settled between them.

For the first time since the bazaar, he felt entirely certain, entirely welcome, entirely at home in her presence. And she—Henrietta—was enjoying Christmas in her own right, choosing joy, choosing herself, and choosing him, too.

Chapter Twenty-Two

C hristmas Eve arrived at last.

The church was alive with quiet anticipation when John arrived with his family, the congregation filling the pews in murmured conversation and occasional bursts of laughter. Snow drifted lazily past the tall windows, softening the world outside, muffling the clatter of late shoppers and the distant bells of horse-drawn trolleys.

John's heart caught as he scanned the faces around him. Each parishioner seemed suffused with the warmth of the season, and therefore eager to greet him—but it was Henrietta he sought. She stood near the choir loft, her posture calm, hands folded neatly over her sheet music. Her cheeks were naturally pink from the warmth of the church, but also from the life that had returned to her after the fever and enforced rest. Her eyes sparkled, reflecting the candlelight, the stained glass, and something else—a quiet confidence he had not fully seen before.

The service continued as planned, and soon, it was time for Henrietta's solo—a graceful replacement for the one she'd lost at the bazaar.

He knew she was still nervous, but she was going through with it nonetheless.

Henrietta inhaled, and John noticed the subtle way she straightened her shoulders, held her chin just so, and let the music rise from her. Her voice was steady, clear, and true, filling the church with the familiar carol, but this time imbued with a softness and strength that made every note seem carefully chosen, every pause deliberate. She was no longer just singing the words; she was conveying the story, the emotion, and the joy of the season itself.

> *O holy night, the stars are brightly shining;*
> *It is the night of the dear Savior's birth.*
> *Long lay the world in sin and error pining,*
> *Till He appeared and the soul felt its worth.*
> *A thrill of hope, the weary world rejoices,*
> *For yonder breaks a new and glorious morn!*
> *Fall on your knees! O hear the angel voices!*
> *O night divine! O night when Christ was born!*
> *O night divine! O night, O night divine!*

John felt himself leaning forward slightly, drawn in by the power of her voice.

He remembered her faltering at the bazaar, how worry and exhaustion had pulled at her every gesture. But tonight, there was none of that strain. Each note was sure, each phrase measured yet vibrant, carrying a warmth that seemed to settle deep in his chest.

For a moment, the world outside—the snow, the noise, the responsibilities—slipped away, leaving only her voice and the quiet ache it stirred in him.

As the final notes trailed off, there was a pause—a breathless, delicate silence—before the congregation broke into soft but reverent applause.

John's eyes followed Henrietta as she bowed slightly, a modest acknowledgment of the applause, her smile small but radiant. Relief and admiration intertwined in him.

Once the service concluded, Henrietta moved through the crowd with ease. John watched as she passed Isaiah Huckabee, who took a half-step forward as if to speak. Henrietta met his gaze for a fraction of a second, her expression polite but utterly remote, and offered the barest, coolest nod of acknowledgment before turning away without breaking her stride. A flush rose to Isaiah's cheeks as he was left standing alone, but she was already gone.

A slow, satisfied smile touched John's lips. He saw the finality in that small gesture—Huckabee clearly understood it, too. Henrietta had scarcely taken another two steps, however, when he saw Mrs. Leland intercept her, speaking with an urgent, frazzled energy and gesturing with a crumpled piece of paper. John felt a familiar tightening in his chest. He saw the familiar pattern: a problem, and Henrietta, the expected solution.

He watched her, expecting to see the flicker of weariness, the dutiful nod he knew so well. But it didn't come. Instead, she smiled calmly, said a few quiet words, and gestured toward another parishioner across the hall.

Mrs. Leland blinked, her frantic energy momentarily deflated. She looked from Henrietta to the other woman, then back again, before giving a quick nod and bustling off in the new direction.

Henrietta didn't watch her go. She simply continued on, her expression serene, her path now taking her directly toward him and his family. A profound sense of pride washed over John, deeper even than what he'd felt during her solo.

When she reached them, she inclined her head in a greeting, her cheeks still flushed from the performance but glowing with warmth. "John," she said softly, voice carrying just enough to be heard over the sounds of the rejoicing congregation, "Merry Christmas Eve."

John's lips parted in a slight, nervous smile. "Merry Christmas Eve, Henrietta. You were extraordinary."

Henrietta's smile deepened, but she gestured subtly to his parents. "I must also greet your family, if you'll permit me."

"Of course."

His father greeted her with a broad smile and a firm handshake. "Miss Miller—or I suppose I should call you *Henrietta*—your solo was remarkable. You have a wonderful voice. And I heard from the pastor that the bazaar raised a record amount for the orphanage this year! A true triumph, thanks in no small part to you and John."

Henrietta's hands folded demurely in front of her. "Thank you, sir. The bazaar is as much John's triumph as mine. And it was a joy to sing tonight—especially after recovering from a few weeks' illness. I am glad to be well enough to participate fully."

John's mother leaned in, her eyes twinkling. "And may I say, you've recovered splendidly. The color in your cheeks is just right, and your voice—it carries so beautifully."

Henrietta inclined her head, acknowledging the compliment, though not without a blush. "I am grateful, Mrs. Baldwin. The rest, and the care of those around me, has done wonders." Her eyes flicked to John with a quiet, unspoken acknowledgment.

Rupert broke away from his gaggle of friends and rushed forward. "Henrietta! That was amazing! John was talking and talking about how amazing you are, but I didn't realize—"

John kicked his brother in the shin.

"Ouch! Johnny! Well, she knows you lo—"

"Rupert," John said, sending his eyes toward the roof of the church and praying for patience. He hadn't actually said the words to Henrietta, and it was best she didn't hear it from his little brother, of all people.

"I'd better find my family," Henrietta said, though not without sending John a mischievous look. "I'll see you later." And she disappeared into the crowd.

His father clapped him on the shoulder. "I'd say that was worth every bit of fuss over notes and schedules."

John inclined his head. "Yes, it is."

Rupert leaned in with a grin. "Are you going to ask to walk her home? Or did you already, you know, plan to do that?"

John shook his head, smiling faintly. "I haven't dared presume anything, Rupert. But perhaps, if the opportunity arises."

His mother's eyes twinkled. "There is time for that, John. Patience is a gift of its own."

As the family finally stepped into the snowy street, John's eyes sought her among the scattering crowd of parishioners heading home.

And there she was—pausing nearby, her family already having left, a small smile on her lips. His heart lifted. She had waited for him. Holding a flat, neatly wrapped parcel he had placed on the pew beside him, he left his family behind and hastened to her side.

A quiet crunch of snow announced footsteps behind Henrietta. As she had hoped, she turned and saw John approaching, his coat dusted with snow, his hands tucked into gloves, eyes bright with anticipation. Even from a distance, there was a warmth in him that almost seemed to defy the bitter December cold.

Her chest lifted in a small, private flutter. It was almost laughable how much she had worried, how many scenarios she had imagined—and now, here he was, exactly as she had hoped, warm and steady against the winter night.

"Henrietta," he said softly, pausing beside her. "I hoped I might find you outside."

Henrietta smiled, a small, private curve of her lips that only he could fully read. "I thought it best to enjoy the snow," she said, glancing up into the flurry of softly falling flakes. "And the quiet. After the service, everything feels so much clearer here. Besides, my aunt and uncle were tired, so they went right home after the service. But I ... wanted a moment to clear my head." A good excuse.

He nodded, following her gaze skyward. "It does. You sang well tonight. Really. I mean it. I didn't realize you had a voice like that—it's a true gift.

She let herself savor the praise, feeling more than just pride in her voice. Tonight, she had sung for herself as much as for anyone else, and it was a gift to be seen beyond her duties and obligations.

"A far better gift, in my mind," he added, "than your uncanny ability to push yourself to the breaking point."

Henrietta chuckled. He was right about that. "That doesn't mean I won't work again, John. I enjoy what I do—within reason. You'll have to understand that."

John just nodded, a serious expression on his face. "I promise to do so, if you can also promise to understand that my work means the world to me, and I take it seriously for a reason. But not, I hope, at the expense of my ... my future."

"And what is your future, John Baldwin?" She turned to him, hands on hips.

John cocked his head. "Why, you, if you'll have me."

Henrietta grinned—and placed a hand on his arm. "Of course I'll have you, John—if you'll have me."

He chuckled, a little self-consciously, and with a light tug, pulled her into his arms. "Is now a good time to say 'I love you, Henrietta Miller'?"

"Only if now is a good time for me to say, 'I love you, John Baldwin,'" Henrietta replied gamely.

John leaned in, capturing her lips in a lingering kiss. Her lips curved into a smile before he even pressed them to hers. This was the certainty she had been craving, the feeling of rightness that stretched quietly through her chest like a warm ribbon. Henrietta's hands found his coat, clutching lightly to anchor herself in the moment. When they finally parted, breathless, Henrietta felt a dizzying combination of delight and relief.

"It must be after midnight by now." John shifted the flat parcel he'd been carrying from under his arm. "I want to give you your Christmas gift."

He placed it in her hands. Her fingers, clumsy from the cold, fumbled with the ribbon. Inside, nestled in tissue paper, lay a new satchel. It was not frivolous or overly ornate, but made of a deep blue, sturdy leather, with a polished brass clasp. It couldn't have been inexpensive, certainly; she could tell he'd found her one made by an expert craftsman. That must have taken time and thought.

"John," she whispered, her voice thick with emotion as she ran a hand over the smooth leather.

"I noticed your other one had served a long and noble career," he teased. "I thought its replacement should be structured, to help with the organization you value." He reached out and opened the flap, showing her the inside, which was cleverly divided into neat compartments. "A place for everything, so you don't have to carry more than you need."

Tears pricked Henrietta's eyes. He wasn't just giving her a gift; he was giving her permission to be unburdened, to carry only what was hers. He was offering his strength not to replace her own, but to support it. "It's the most thoughtful gift I have ever received," she said softly.

"Good," he murmured. "Because I intend for it to last a very long time." He leaned in, resting his forehead briefly against hers before he stepped back. "I should take you home."

"I know." Sighing, she released her grip and stepped back. Together, they walked down the lane in the swirling snow. And Henrietta realized something—something absolutely shocking. For the first time in she didn't know how long, she didn't feel burdened by anything. She felt … joyful.

Tonight, she was simply herself, enjoying the peace she had earned, and sharing it with him.

A Note from the Author

Dear Reader,

Thank you for taking the time to read John and Henrietta's story! I hope you enjoyed it. If you feel so led, feel free to leave a review on your favorite platform. Even a few words are helpful, whatever your opinions on this story might be. Reviews help indie authors like me reach the right readers.

With John and Henrietta, I didn't want to just write the same old story of two enemies who are both taking exact opposite approaches to trying to organize a Christmas bazaar. That felt too typically Hallmark-ish to me. Instead, I decided to focus in on two workaholics navigating their separate (but oddly very similar approaches) to work and volunteering.

I hope this story blessed you and reminded you that the greatest hope we have is not in ourselves, or in our ability to manage our lives or our work or our calling, but in Christ Himself, in His will for our lives. He is the ultimate organizer, and we have no need to exert our own will on our lives when He has already so beautifully crafted the story, in a way we could never even have dream of ... a better way.

Interested in joining my email list and receiving a free novella and monthly border collie pictures? You can do so by heading to https:// kellynrothauthor.com/and entering your email address. I would love to get to know you there!

TTFN!

~Kellyn Roth